Jacob Marley's
Christmas Carol

Jacob Marley's

Christmas Carol

Tom Mula

ADAMS PUBLISHING
Holbrook, Massachusetts

Published by Adams Media Corporation
260 Center Street, Holbrook, MA 02343

ISBN: 1-55850-537-7
Printed in the United States of America

First Edition
J   I   H   G   F   E   D   C   B   A

Library of Congress Cataloging-in-Publication Data
Mula, Tom.
Jacob Marley's Christmas carol / Tom Mula.—1st ed.
          p.   cm.
ISBN 1-55850-537-7 (hb)
1. Dickens, Charles. 1812–1870—Characters—
Jacob Marley—Fiction.   I. Title.
PS3563.U3867J33   1995
813'.54—dc20
95-38108
CIP

This book is available at quantity discounts for bulk purchases.
For information, call 1-800-872-5627.

with thanks to:
Steve Scott, Tom Creamer, and Chuck Smith;
to
Sheldon Patinkin, Terry McCabe, Kriyananda,
and Ron Nolte;
to
Dale Calandra, Shifra Werch, Pauline Brailsford,
Bill Norris, Greg Vinkler, Christine Thatcher,
Mary Ernster, Dev Kennedy,
and Nicole Hollander;
to
Roche Schulfer, Bob Falls, Cindy Bandle, Julie Massey,
Bill Williams, Mara Tapp,
Brandon Toropov, Ed Walters,
and
Cathy O'Malley;
to
Mom and Dad;
to
Charles Dickens;
and to
Hazel Flowers–McCabe,
who first observed that Marley got a raw deal.

for
Kerry Wayne,
my own personal bogle

~ An Apology ~

With *A Christmas Carol*, Charles Dickens created one of the great modern myths, with a lesson we all need to hear, again and again: that hope is possible, and that we can change for the better.

For the last five years, it has been my great privilege to play Scrooge in the Goodman Theatre's excellent production of Tom Creamer's splendid adaptation of Dickens's book. This has been one of the great joys of my life.

During the course of those several hundred performances, the injustice of Marley's fate (to have arranged, somehow, for Scrooge to be visited by the spirits of Christmas Past, Present, and Future, and yet to have no hope of his own redemption) seemed more and more unfair to me. This book is an attempt to right that injustice.

I approach Dickens's masterpiece with fear and trembling, but I take comfort in the knowledge that however this effort is received, *A Christmas Carol* will remain pristine, unbesmirched by *my* muddy little foot-prints.

But, hopefully, there will be one less sad old ghost clanking about through eternity.

arley was dead, to begin with. There is no doubt whatever about that. Marley was dead. This must be distinctly understood, or nothing wonderful can come of the story I am about to relate. I must repeat: Old Jacob Marley was thoroughly, unequivocally, irrevocably dead, and a good thing, too. In the words of an old song, "He was not only merely dead, he was really most sincerely dead."

So, imagine his surprise to find himself, shortly after breathing his wretched last (and fully expecting the next sight that he beheld to have something to do with brimstone), in a dark, dusty,

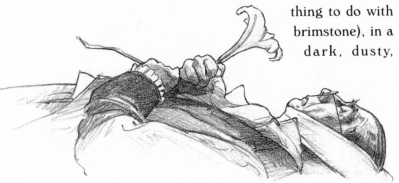

ill-swept hallway, littered with old rags and scraps of paper. Far ahead of him at the end of the hallway, a light flickered dimly behind the frosted glass of a closed door. Marley looked over his shoulder; behind him was only darkness, absolute and impenetrable. So, not knowing what else to do, he began to shuffle his way through the litter towards the light at the door.

The hallway, as I said, was dark, being windowless save for the one at the end. Yet as Marley walked, he felt a slight, clammy breeze against his face, a little like questioning fingers. And why did he think that he heard whispering? He looked—there was no one there but himself. But what was that rustling in the papers behind him? Marley walked a little faster, until he heard, he was sure, a rasping, whispered laugh just behind him at his collar, and felt what must surely be something clutching at his ankles—and then he traveled the rest of the distance to the door very quickly indeed.

There was no name above the door, no name on the glass, and even with his spectacles, Marley could see nothing through the window but the light of a single candle flickering half-heartedly in the room beyond. He hesitated outside the door to consider his options, and to wonder if he had any.

"Haven't got all day," said a voice from inside.

Marley put his hand to the knob, and went in. "Where the devil am I?" he demanded.

A laugh. "Oh, no, my dear sir, nothing of that kind, I assure you. Come in, sir, come in. All are welcome here."

He found himself in a small office, filled to overflowing with old books and ledgers. The shelves on the walls were piled with books, the cabinets crammed with books, and towers of books tottered dangerously everywhere. A rough path had been cleared from the door to the single desk in the room, where the office's sole occupant sat, poring over a ledger. He peered at Marley over his spectacles.

"Name?" The occupant of the room was an ancient, rather bulldoggish little man, about the size and shape of a small chair. He was worn and padded and antiquely dressed, with long white hair floating distractedly about his shoulders.

"I beg your pardon?" said Marley frostily.

"Name. Your name, sir." The man's spectacles flashed in the candlelight. "Come, come, this is one of the easy ones. They only get harder from here on."

"Marley," said Jacob, now fully annoyed.

"Full?"

"What?"

"Full name, if you please."

"Jacob Quimby Marley. I demand to know where I am."

"All in good time, sir, all in good time. Sit down, if you wish. That pile there."

Marley sat, simmering.

It's time we took a good look at the man our story concerns. Sorry. Marley was a proper, tight, dry, pruny old thing. He looked like someone had wound him one turn too tight, or perhaps like someone had sucked all the juice out of him long ago and left only a desiccated rind. His face was frozen in sour disapproval, as if he had bitten into a lemon by mistake and hadn't liked it much. There was no color about the man; he was as gray and colorless as a shadow, except for the reddish flash in his eyes when he was angry.

And he was angry now. More than anything else, he hated not being totally in control. All of his wretched life had been a clawing scramble to the top of the heap, to mastery, and Marley had commanded respect, at least; his dignity was a formidable suit of armor against the world. Most people feared him. Those who could, avoided him. Those who couldn't, postponed the ordeal for as long as possible, and then got it over as quickly as they could. Marley liked that.

Marley had spent the last thirty years sitting behind an intimidating desk at Scrooge & Marley. Scrooge & Marley (Scrooge was Marley's partner; unfortunately, more about *that* one later) was a firm whose primary business was putting other people's money into its own pockets. It did this by selling them things (dry goods mostly), by investing, which is a way of earning money from other people's work, and by loaning desperate people money at usurious rates. For years Marley had sat at his desk like a dry old spider, knowing that sooner or later, another luckless fly would blunder into his web.

But now that was over, and Marley teetered on a pile of ledgers, waiting—for what, he didn't know.

"Let me see, Marley, Marley—that's "M" isn't it? I believe you're sitting on the M's. That one beside you, if you please." Marley snorted; he would never have tolerated such disorder in his office. The man looked at him expectantly; Marley realized he was expected to hand him the book. Marley looked at his fingernails. If this fellow wanted it so badly, he could just get it himself—Jacob Marley wasn't any man's clerk. For a few moments, they sat unmoving, just looking at each other. Then the old man sighed, came off the stool behind his desk, and walked over to where Marley sat. Marley saw that he walked with some pain, supporting himself by leaning on things. Well, he should keep his office in better order. The old man bent to retrieve the book, and took it back to his desk.

It was a large, brown, leather-bound book, well-worn and a little shabby, with "Manders through Mintington" penned on the binding. "Manning, Mappleton, Marjoe," he said, turning the pages. "Ah, here we are. Marley, Jacob Q—oh. Oh my." He was silent for a time, reading. He turned a disquieting number of pages. "So that was you, was it? Hmmph. They hadn't told me you were coming." He took off his spectacles and rubbed his eyes for a moment, then looked up at Marley. "Well, you have been busy, haven't you?"

"Enough of this. Who are you, sir? Where am I?"

"Oh, look about you. You know where you are. You're a businessman. This is the Counting House."

Marley's blood, never very warm to begin with, chilled.

But he didn't show it, not a bit. If this was to be a business transaction, a negotiation of some kind, he had been there many times before, and he wasn't about to be taken advantage of. He looked at his interviewer sternly.

"And what's all this about?"

"Well, Mr. Marley, simply put, I'm afraid you've come up short in your accounts." He looked down at the book, and turned several pages. "Your debits, sir, are great." He turned several more pages, quite a few, actually. "Very great." Then he peered down at the book and rubbed it for a moment, as if trying to remove a smudge. He pulled out a magnifying glass and bent over close, squinting at something small. "And your credits—almost non-existent."

"What are you talking about, man? Speak plainly."

"Your contract, sir. You haven't fulfilled your contract."

"Contract? What do you mean? I never entered into a contract with you, sir."

"Oh, yes, you did. Well, not with me precisely, but with those I represent, yes."

"You're not dealing with a fool, man. I know what I've signed or haven't signed, and I never signed any contract with you. Just exactly what is the nature of this purported document?"

"Oh, the usual. A loan, really."

Marley barked a scornful laugh. "You made a loan to me?" This was beginning to be amusing. "How much?"

"The usual. But you have exhausted your account, squandered it, if you will, and now you must settle, sir."

"Claptrap. This is rubbish. I can't be held to a contract I've never signed, never even seen. I demand that you produce this imaginary ... "

"As you wish." From a file behind him, the old man pulled out a document, and unfolded it. It was quite official looking, of a standard legal size and form, sealed and notarized—all very proper. He handed it to Marley.

"We'll soon get to the bottom of this." Marley pulled down his spectacles and started to read.

~

He read for quite some time and as he read, the paper began to shake a bit in his hand. His face dropped its mask of disdain, and became solemn, even a little sad. When he had finished, he let the paper fall into his lap, and covered his eyes with his hand.

"Why—why wasn't I made aware of this?"

"Oh, you were, my dear sir, many times, on many occasions. But you chose to ignore them. In fact, you were quite extraordinarily obstinate about it."

Marley looked down for a moment and swallowed several times. Then he looked up hopefully, as if he had remembered something. "I thought we were to be forgiven our debts ... "

The old man grinned at him. "Not my department, my dear sir. Here, all is paid to the last farthing."

"What's to become of me now?"

"The usual. What did you do, time upon time, when someone defaulted on a loan?"

Marley spread his hands helplessly. "Well, we had no recourse but to ... their assets, I suppose, were occasionally ... seized."

"Well, we can't very well do that, can we? You haven't any."

"Well, what then?"

"Why, debtor's' prison, I suppose. I'm sorry, but it's the law." The old man spread his hands in mocking imitation of Marley. "Not my doing, I assure you. Really, quite out of my hands."

Suddenly Marley felt his arms pulled down, and a great weight upon his legs. He looked down, and saw great iron chains hanging from his hands, his arms, his ankles, his neck. Fastened to the chains were leases and contracts, ledger books and cash boxes, past-due receipts and, most of all, locks—locks of all kinds, steel and iron, rusty and new, tiny toy locks such as a child might have used, and great, heavy steel locks big as a man's head, that might have been used to secure the vaults of an empire.

"What are these?"

"You wear the chains you forged in life, Mr. Marley. Is their pattern strange to you? Know that you made them, link by link, yard by yard, cash box by cash box."

Marley tried to move, to raise his arms, and the chains moved with him with a life of their own, like great heavy arms and hands clamped about his ankles and limbs, iron clamps, cold and biting.

Terror seized old Marley's heart, cold and biting like iron, too. He raised his arms and the chains moved too, floating in a great tangle before his eyes. Marley fell to his knees.

"Mercy! Please, please, kind sir, I beg of you—have some mercy!"

From the other, only smiling silence.

Then a wind began to rise in the room, first just stirring the papers and the covers of the books. It sniffed around Marley's ankles first, and then, having found him, encircled him in earnest, whirling about him faster and faster, howling in his ears, shrieking, stronger and stronger, lifting him off the ground, almost.

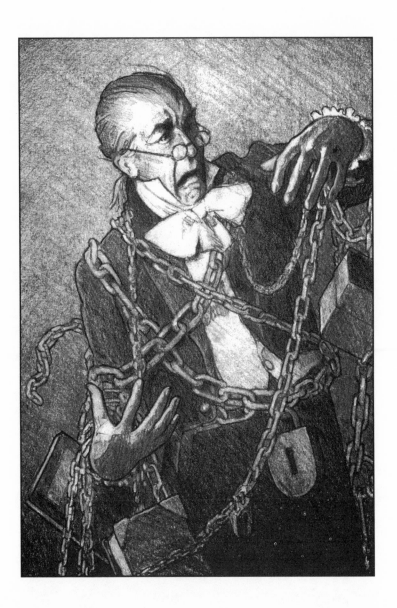

Then the old man stood up from behind his desk, and stood, and stood, and stood; for as he stood, he grew, and kept growing, and increasing in brightness, until he was an immense, shining figure tall as a cathedral and blazing like the sun, "robed in glory," as they say, with in his hand—what? A sword? A scale? The light was really too bright to tell. Marley covered his eyes.

The old man's voice changed and, though big as the sea now, seemed gentler. "And now, Mr. Marley, learn what you ought to have learned. See what you should have seen, feel what you should have felt; for no one escapes these lessons, and since you failed to learn them the easier way, now you must learn them in a more difficult way. I pray for your sake you learn them here, for the next way is more difficult, still."

"Now go—and let's see if we can do a little better, shall we?"

And Marley felt himself lifted by the wind, being whirled, tossed, blown like a dead leaf, and hurled out into the night sky, and the watching, silent stars.

❧ Chapter Two ❧

Darkness, piercing cold, blackness relieved only by the icy twinkle of distant stars.

The wind was cold, wet cold—a vicious, heart-stopping, bone-snapping cold. Alone now, Marley howled in the wind, howled his anguish to the silent stars. The wind whipped Marley, chained and howling, through the night sky.

He saw before him a dot of light in the darkness. It grew and grew, becoming, he saw, a globe, a ball of swirling colors suspended against the black velvet. It continued to grow at an alarming rate, and he realized that he was hurtling towards it, and that it was immense. As he grew closer he saw that the globe was surrounded by a thin membrane, an air, an atmosphere. And as he grew closer still, he saw that the membrane appeared to move; indeed, it did move, for the atmosphere surrounding the jewel-like globe was alive. It writhed with life; every molecule danced with life and intention; the very air breathed, and sang.

For the air was peopled. He saw, approaching, that it was full of half-transparent people—spirits floating in the air, suspended, as if at the bottom of the sea. Some plummeted through the atmosphere, shrieking, like comets; some swam by more slowly; but most merely floated, eddying in the currents of the air like seaweed, allowing themselves to drift, to be carried, not caring where. The cloud of souls seemed limitless—as far as Marley could see, there were only more spirits, and more—quite literally, the air was spirited. Spirits from all times, in all manner of costumes, floated below him.

The wind that was driving him slowed, and Marley found himself at the outer edge, the topmost stratum of this spirit world. Here all was silence, and the people were motionless, frozen, eerily still, floating in the air like drowned men at the bottom of the sea. Some were in chairs, or standing, and some were even reclining on the empty air; but each was alone, and well apart from the others, as solitary and separate as statues or portraits on a wall, staring off into space, unseeing, as if dreaming or lost in thought.

The nearest was a sad-looking young man whose long hair floated in the air above his head. He was sitting in a stained old armchair. Marley stopped before him.

"Please, sir, can you help me? Where are we? What are we doing here?"

The man looked up, and for a moment, regarded Marley detachedly. Then he began to laugh. At first his laughter was merely awful—a dry, unsmiling chuckle that a spider might have laughed. Then a sort of joyless, choking, gurgling sound came from his throat. Then it became something like barking. And then something like a scream. And after that, his laughter was horrible, a terrible thing to watch—face spasmed a mottled purple, spittle flying, eyes and veins popping, hands clenched, nails digging into the flesh. The laughter was taken up by the others around him, until everyone within sight was howling, screaming, eyes clenched, hands knotted, heads thrown back, howling, entire faces transformed into howling, toothy mouths.

The shrieking tore into his skull like an iron spike. Marley clapped his fettered hands to his ears, trying to shut out the awful sound, but he couldn't. With all his heart he wished to be elsewhere; then all was blackness.

～

"Oh, the bells of hell go ting-a-ling-a-ling ... " Marley awoke with a start. He was relieved to find that he had been transported to some part of this hellish world where he was essentially alone, except that someone was singing in his ear.

Literally, *in* his ear. For though Marley could see no one, the annoying buzzing persisted, and seemed to be coming from his right ear, as if something had crawled in there while he was unconscious.

"When was the last time you cleaned in here, old prune? Dis-*gusting*. Well, at least we won't have to wax in here. Ooo—yuck. And carpeted. We *must* have some discussions about hygiene."

Marley hopped about with his finger in his ear, trying to dislodge the offender.

"If you'll take your bloody big finger—bleaugh. Nails could use some work, too—out of my front hallway, I'll come out." Marley did.

A tiny man all made of light about the size of a raisin flew out of his ear and floated in the air before him.

Marley made a determined swat at the offender, and was heartily disappointed to see his hand pass entirely through the insect without any visible effect, except to set the little man dancing before him in a vulgar way.

"It's no good swinging at me, I'm afraid, and I wouldn't do it any more if I were you. You'll just tangle up your chains, and they're the very devil to undo."

Reluctantly, Marley paused to examine his companion. Floating in the air before him, about eye-level, was a glowing figure—about the size of a healthy bird dropping,

Marley thought. On closer examination still, he saw grinning back at him the same sour face he'd seen in the mirror for the last quarter-century—the same pinched nostrils, tight, disapproving lips, et cetera— complete with a tiny pigtail, spectacles perched upon his forehead—and wearing chains like himself.

"Who the hell are you?"

"Who do I look like? Do you think I would choose to look like this, given a choice?"

No one had talked to Jacob Marley like this for a long time. "Well, um, you look like me."

"Brilliant. Eternity's going to be a long, long time."

Marley paused. He had been thinking exactly the same thing. "So who are you? Are you some sort of devil, sent to torment me?"

"Devil is such a hurtful word, don't you think? And imprecise. The correct terminology is *numen* or *genius*, but the word I prefer is 'bogle'." That's B-O-G-L-E, bogle. It's an old word, somewhat out of usage now, but with a sort of charm, don't you think? But what you call me isn't really so important; I want you to think of me as your welcoming committee, your guide to your new home."

"New home, eh? And is this hell, then?"

"Oh, clean out your ears, old prune. (And I *do* mean that.) This is 'debtor's prison.' Never did listen to anybody, did you? Might try it, for a change."

"I thank you, sir, for your advice," Marley grunted. "And I believe I've spent quite enough time listening to you. Good day." And Marley turned, intending to go somewhere, anywhere away from this ...

"Where are we going?" The insect was bobbing before his face once more.

"*We* are not going anywhere. Don't you have some pressing business that demands your presence elsewhere?"

"Nope. You are my business, old pudding. Would it were not so. But we don't have much say in these matters, you and I. Bound together, we are, I'm afraid. Conjoined and conjunct. Birds of a feather. Peas in a pod. Siamese twins ... "

Marley ground his teeth a bit; he was beginning to appreciate the idea of damnation. "So I am to be burdened with your company forever, then?"

"Burdened? I like that. Believe me, the 'pleasure' is all mine. In fact, I believe I have the worse part of the bargain: I've gotten to stand beside you for years and years already, and watch you becoming the fine specimen that you are now; you, at least, have been ignorant of me for that time."

"Well, it appears that both of our luck's run out."

"An understatement, given the circumstances."

"What now?"

"Well, we could do the grand tour. You know, poke

about, get the feel of the place. After all, you're going to be here a long, long time."

They began to move through the ether.

~

"The greatest punishment here is the company, I'm afraid. No one wants to talk about anything but themselves, and of course, no one wants to listen to anything else, either. It gets very tiresome, very quickly."

"Doesn't sound so bad to me," said Marley.

"For eternity? Think about it. Think about the worst headache you've ever had—the one that went on and on for days and days. Remember how time seemed to stop and just sort of throb there between your eyes? Well, welcome to eternity. Only here, it really *does* go on forever."

"Thank you so much for clarifying that for me."

"That's my job. But the thing everyone seems to forget is that time doesn't really exist, anyway. It's strictly a human construct—sort of an imaginary, collective filing system. It's not a real thing; people just like lists. It's tidier. But you know, you're looking a little depressed. Let's look about, shall we?" The little man waved his arm and the two of them moved downwards.

~

"Dante had it wrong. Or rather, like most artists, he embellished it too much. His sinners were operatic— betrayers of empires, pederastic popes. It's not like that at all, or at least it wasn't until you got here."

Marley ignored his companion and looked about him. This world did seem to be constructed in layers, each layer made up of sinners of a particular sort. The layer where he currently found himself was fantastic: All around him beings of nightmare floated by on the currents of air like exotic sea creatures. Marley felt like he was imprisoned in some hellish aquarium.

He was surrounded by others like himself, bound as he was, yet not altogether identically. One man was chained to a pack of yapping dogs; another to a dining-table piled high with rotting food; another to flame-like images of ladies, laughing, their mouths open showing rotten teeth. There were many of these spirits around him, each bound to something; but what really horrified Marley were the creatures that were no longer human, and yet still lived—a pile of rags and bones and antique clothes that moved and gestured as if alive; a scarecrow of notes and papers in the shape of a man; wardrobes and treasure-boxes with hands and faces that called to him, beckoning. He saw a woman, a lady of society with whom he had had some business dealings. She was draped in jewels, nearly covered in them; but as she floated past him, nodding a greeting, he realized that he couldn't differentiate the woman from her jewelry—it seemed as if the bangles and necklaces were growing from her, had embedded themselves, gnawed their way into her skin, and the flesh around them was sore and ragged-looking.

"Yes, they grow together, eventually. Inseparable. Each becomes the thing he loves, in a way. Or hates. Those are the ones that are most amusing—people bound forever to what they most despised in life, continually trying to escape, but literally joined at the hip. Most entertaining. By the way, you'll look fine as an animated pile of sovereigns and assorted loose change ... "

Marley was revulsed. A looking-glass floated by, with a pale face inside, pressed against the glass, scratching to get out. A man with books growing out of him; you could just see his eyes, trapped, peering over the volume that had attached itself, sucking, to his face. Many, many gin and wine bottles with little, shrunken, pickled-looking people in them, scrabbling weakly at the sides, trying to get out. Most seemed blinded, ignorant of their companions in the ether that carried them all; but some swam together, grown together like the limbs of a tree, forever quarreling, bickering, clawing at one another, yet bound to each other as strong as iron. Some women wore their children about their necks and waists like decorations, tiny, wasted, and starved looking; some men carried their mothers or fathers grown onto their backs like the old man of the sea. Many others had grown into things like furniture; one unfortunate man dragged his house about with him; another, an entire government.

And the sound was intense. The air was filled with din of all kinds: of argument, of complaint, of bargaining and pleading; of anger and threats, storming against unseen tormentors and unjust fate; of anger turned inwards, self-directed, anguished. Each soul seemed imprisoned in its own pain as if locked in the cell of a madhouse, with neighbors screaming all around; and each soul confronted its own pain, alone.

Marley was horrified. His companion, seeing this, took pity on him and led him away. "Come, let's see some more," he said gently. "It's not all like this."

Of course he was right. It was worse.

The bogle led Marley through various levels. Some were levels of pleading, some of rage, some of sorrow. In some, the souls tried to hurt themselves, or others. Some levels were filled with a constant shrieking; others, with only a low moaning. The worst was the topmost level, the one Marley had entered when he had first arrived. Here the anguish became silence and darkness and cold, and each soul was completely, utterly alone. This was the level of despair; here, indeed, all hope was abandoned, and from here souls blinked out, disappeared as if a very small, dim candle had finally guttered out.

"Where do they go?" asked Marley.

The bogle seemed uncomfortable here, seemed in a hurry to leave. "Don't know, old thing," he said. "Nobody talks about it much. Maybe nowhere."

"You mean they just vanish and reappear?"

"No, I mean they go *nowhere*—they cease to exist. Become *nothing*."

"Sounds like a relief."

"You might think that now," the bogle said, looking at Marley seriously. "But no—this ... It's never discussed. This rejection, utter annihilation ... " The bogle shuddered, unable to go on. "Let's get away from here."

～

They continued on. Throughout the rest of the tour, Marley's guide watched him carefully. As they traveled, Marley became progressively quieter and quieter, and finally quite still. "How do you like your new home?"

Marley sat down on the empty air and put his head in his hands

"Something the matter?" buzzed the little man.

"Go away."

"You're not letting this depress you, are you?"

Marley did not answer.

"I do have something else to show you. Come."

"No. No more. Show me where I am to go, and I'll go there, but leave me alone."

"Really, you should see this."

"No thank you."

"Sorry to insist, old pustule, but come you must. We're going home."

And the little spirit waved his arm, and Marley was propelled down, down through layer upon layer of the spirit world to the living surface of the earth below.

~

It was London, on a crisp market morning at the fish market in Billingsgate. The streets and alleys close by the river were crowded with shouting, whistling, singing, and swearing men. Barrows of fish, scales glistening in the morning light, were unloaded and passed up the steps from the boats, slopping water on the steps of stone. Costermongers and oyster-wives, brokers and salesmen, fishers unloading their catch, and buyers from all levels of life, pushed and elbowed and cursed and laughed. The air itself sparkled with the cold, and men and boys huddled about the few barrels of open coals, or the coffee-sellers' wagons, warming their hands and faces, dancing and winking and slapping themselves to stay warm. The tremendous noise they made, the confusion, the din, the tumult was awesome, and, in a way, somehow splendid and grand.

Marley sneered, as he and his spirit-guide looked down on the crowd. All his life Jacob Marley had striven to distance and separate himself from the common throng, to keep his hands clean of their dirt and sweat and smell; he prided himself on having risen above it. Now he literally floated in the air above their heads; he no longer had to touch and mingle, to shoulder and nudge and shove among them. Now he was truly of a higher plane.

"Disgusting, ain't it?" shouted his little companion, perching near his ear. "Messy. How can they live like that? Each in the other's face, each in the other's business, hands-on, bad smells, fingerprints—like some big, damn, noisy, meddling, intrusive fam—"

"Why are we here?" Marley cut him off. "I don't see what's to be gained here. I've seen all this before."

"Have you? Well, perhaps you never noticed *this*." The bogle waved his hand.

Marley felt a bit dizzy, felt a change in his eyes, and, as he blinked, hard, to clear his vision, the world before him doubled, tripled in population. For beside every man there stood a spirit, if not two or three, above him, beside him, at his shoulder, at his elbow; some watching in horror, others bemused, others helping, laughing, whispering encouragement—all interested, caring, all intensely involved. The world was filled—not only with human inhabitants, but with spirit visitors. The streets were crowded with corporeal and non-corporeal forms, floating above, mingling with, being jostled and walked-through and tossed about in the tumult of passing humanity. Marley gaped, astonished.

"Crowded, what?"

"What are they doing?"

"Nothing, most of them. Just watching. Spectators at the cricket match, cheering the home team. Others, offering a little help, occasionally; a bright idea, a kind word, a pat on the back. Holding hands, sometimes. Listening. Encouraging."

"Did I have ... help ... companions like that?"

"Legions. You were a special project."

"I wasn't aware ... "

"That's an understatement. At one time, there were literally one hundred and thirty-eight angels dancing on the head of your particular pin, but you outlasted them. Finally, they all got discouraged and went on to other, more promising projects—ax-murderers and the like. Unfortunately, I was stuck."

Marley, stung, whirled on the little man. "Well, I never asked for your company! Consider yourself unstuck! I release you! If you're so unhappy, go! Begone! I liberate you. Trouble yourself no longer. You're free."

The little man sighed a very deep sigh. "Not so easy, old pudding. I'm yours. I'm here for the duration."

He paused to say something, then thought better of it. "Let's go for a walk."

~

And walk they did, in their way, through the streets and alleys toward the center of town, sometimes floating above the crowds, sometimes on the ground among them. Once in a narrow passageway, Marley stopped directly in front of a man selling second-hand hats and scarves, expecting the man to humbly bob his head and give way. But the man walked through him, unseeing, and for a moment Marley was overwhelmed, first with the heat of the man's body, then with the racket and jumble of the man's thoughts, concerns, worries, and needs. The man walked on, leaving Marley disoriented and shaking his head, trying to sort the man's thoughts from his own. It was most unpleasant, and from then on, Marley tried to keep out of the way, to keep from being touched and passed-through, but he couldn't. For from then on, his companion seemed deliberately to steer him through the narrowest paths and alleyways, so that Marley was constantly being elbowed, ignored, and walked-through; for some reason, the little spirit seemed to find this amusing, and chuckled to himself in a most annoying way.

Sometimes Marley stopped before a particular face, inches away, and studied it as if trying to read something written in a foreign tongue. Once they stopped before a little girl, pink and pretty despite her dirt and cast-off rags, sitting on a doorstep and singing to quiet the baby in her arms. Marley stood before her a good while; he was quite surprised when she looked up and their eyes met. She considered him solemnly, then smiled shyly at him and returned her attention to the child. Marley found this unsettling.

"Yes, some of them can see us a little, or otherwise know that we're here."

Marley frowned and was silent. They moved on.

~

They arrived at the great square before St. Paul's. The sun was setting into blue-gray twilight and the air had grown biting, but the square bustled with people. "Come," said the little spirit. "Bet you've never seen it from here." And the two of them floated up and up, finally perching on the cathedral's great dome to look down at the square below.

The city was awesome, spread out before them as far as the eye could see: red clouds to the west catching the last of the sun's rays, the lights of London beginning to twinkle against the dark, a couple of stars shining faintly in the East, night coming on. From where they watched the square teemed with figures ...

"Like ants," said Marley. "Insects."

"You would say that, wouldn't you? Seem small, do they? Trivial? Insignificant?"

"No, that's not it. They seem so ... temporal. Temporary. Fragile. All thinking they're going to live forever, not knowing that ... Yet—cheerful. Sort of brave, in a way."

"Whistling in the graveyard, eh? Well, that's the truth. Watch this." The little man did something else to Marley's eyes, and he saw, standing beside each man, woman, and child in the square, a tall figure all in black, robed and hooded, with its face hidden.

Marley chilled. "Who are they?"

The little man grinned. "Don't you recognize Him? You had a visit from Him not so very long ago."

"You mean ... "

"Exactly."

"Oh."

"Don't remember, eh? Mind you, I'm not surprised. Most choose not to remember much about their passing."

They watched in silence for a while the crowds in the square, each accompanied, unawares, by a grim companion. "Is ... are They there all the time?"

"Every day, first to last, that figure walks beside every man on the globe."

"And they never see Him until ... "

"Um-hmm. Until it's time."

"Ah." Marley was quiet for a while

"Changes things, don't it? Probably a lot of them would do things a bit differently, if they knew What walked beside them."

"Perhaps."

"Catch in your throat? Getting a cold?"

"Oh, shut up."

～

They returned to the spirit world and Marley sat mid-air, gloomily rubbing at a place on his wrist where one of his chains had begun to burrow into the skin. "So what do I do now?" he asked.

"What do you mean?"

"So now I just stay here until I look like one of them?" he said, indicating a group of phantoms that floated past, grown together into a mass of arms, fingers, claws, eternally stretched out to grasp something eternally beyond their reach.

"Up to you, old crumpet. It's certainly an option. Or, you could drift about feeling sorry for yourself and put-upon, sucking on your regrets like some nasty lozenge. Growing more private, more solitary, and darker, until finally your light goes out. You could do that if you like."

"If I like? You speak as if I have a choice."

"You do."

"I thought I was here forever."

"If you choose. It's up to you. You can stay if you like. Most people do."

"Choose to stay here? In this torment?"

"Most do. It's comfortable. It's what they're used to, for although their torments are grotesque, they're familiar and thus comfy, in a way. Most do stay, for it's a great trouble to change enough to go somewhere else."

"You mean I don't have to stay?" For the first time in a great while Marley's face was lit with a kind of hope.

"No, you're not stuck—no one is stuck anywhere. It's just that in certain places it's harder to move—harder to move yourself, that is. Look at that man over there." Marley saw a man sitting glumly, half-submerged in a moldy armchair, shrouded in gloom and silence, staring at nothing. "That man has sat just like that for nearly a hundred years, and each moment he stays like that decreases the possibility of his changing, ever. Each man constructs his own particular hell—some are quite ingenious. He has fashioned his rut and is now pretty much stuck in it, but no one has put him there, no one keeps him there but himself."

"You mean we don't have to stay here?" said Marley, nearly roaring now.

"Of course not!"

"Well, how do we get out?"

"You apply for a transfer, of course."

~

"Mr. Marley, delighted to see you again," said the old record-keeper. "Your paperwork appears to be in order. I trust your accommodations were satisfactory? I hear you've been making yourself quite at home."

"Most amusing. I'm here to apply for a transfer."

"So I understood. You are aware, of course, that there are certain requirements that must be met ... "

"I'll sign anything. Just get me out of here."

"But there are ... "

"I have no interest in spending eternity in this dreary hole of an office chatting with you! You have my paperwork before you. Now, what's next?"

The old man regarded Marley evenly. "I'm happy to see that your reputation has not been exaggerated. But I don't believe you understand the gravity of what you propose to do; the difficulty ... "

"I don't care! Just get me out of here! What do I have to sign? What do I have to do?"

"Very well." The old man spoke to Marley's small companion, who was perched on an inkwell. "I gather you have not quite given him all the particulars of his situation?"

"Oh, I showed him around, all right, and explained the basics."

"But the specifics of his task, his request ... ?"

The bogle shrugged. "I tried to explain it to him, but you can see how he is. Let's just surprise him."

The old man chuckled a bit, then composed himself, and addressed Marley. "Well, Mr. Marley, you have your work cut out for you. Sign here, if you please." Marley signed in a fever, not bothering to read what he signed. "And here." He signed again. "And also here." Again. "And here." One last time. The old man handed him a copy. "Here is your assignment."

Marley looked at the paper and blanched dead white. "No one told me ... "

"So I gather. But that's how things are done here. I wish you luck."

—

"SCROOGE? I have to redeem old Scrooge? The one man I knew who was worse than I was? Impossible! I'll never be able to ... "

"Fitting, I think. After all, the two of you were a nearly identical pair of gargoyles."

"We were not. He was much worse!"

"That's not what the record says. But let me see this contract. 'Party of the first part, blah, blah, blah.'"

The little man floated above the agreement. The contract was ornately hand-written in a gothic script, and
signed with an indecipherable sign that reminded Marley
of the smell of orange-rind and the way sunlight looked
on the water. "Here we are. 'On effecting a Total and
Complete Change of Heart on the said subject, Mr. E.
Scrooge; (said Change must be Willing and Irreversible);
on the effecting of such Change, all Debts shall be
Forgiven, all Bonds Broken, and the undersigned' (you,

old thing, I assume) 'shall be freed to seek his Greater Joy.' What do they mean, 'Change of Heart?' That's not very specific. That could mean anything. And 'Greater Joy?' That couldn't be more vague. This would never hold up in a court of law."

"This is terrible. A willing and irreversible change of heart—it's not possible. He doesn't have one."

"And listen to this: 'This Contract shall expire in Twenty-Four Hours, Earth-Time, from the moment of signature, or Cock's Crow, whichever shall come sooner.'"

"Ridiculous! If I had twenty-four years, perhaps, but twenty-four hours ... "

"Well, nobody said it would be easy."

"But this—it can't be done! It ... it's not fair!"

"Stop whining. You're the one who wanted to do this. Actually, these work-release things are in great demand. You're lucky to get one."

"And this is my only chance of getting out of here?"

"Quite."

"Hell."

"You could say that. Well, you'd best get moving. Twenty-four hours isn't very long. Time's a-wasting."

"I suppose you're right. Well, how do we go about it?"

"That's up to you."

"Up to me? I thought you were here to help me."

"Oh, I'm allowed to facilitate, but the inspiration and the perspiration must be yours. Don't you love that? 'The inspiration and the per ... '"

"Delightful." Marley sighed a resigned sigh. "Well, I suppose we'd best begin by paying a visit to the old crocodile."

"Couldn't do any harm to take a look."

"This is Scrooge we're talking about."

"Indeed. Sorry, I forgot."

Chapter Three

"CRATCHIT!"

The windows of the counting house rattled, and a few icicles shattered on the cobblestones outside.

"Yes, Mr. Scrooge?"

Marley found himself back in the counting house of the firm Scrooge and Marley. Little had changed. Cratchit, their clerk, still shivered in his dank little closet off the main room; Scrooge, old booger, had appropriated the larger office, of course, and taken over Marley's desk. Otherwise, all was the same, and Marley felt some comfort to find himself at home. For a while he browsed contentedly, floating among the open ledger-books, the files, and the reassuringly full cash boxes inside the safe.

Now, if you thought Marley was bad, well, Scrooge—hmm. Another story-teller described him in exorbitant detail; suffice to say that in no way did he exaggerate. "A squeezing, wrenching, grasping, clutching, covetous old sinner," describes Ebenezer Scrooge rather more kindly than he deserves.

"Yes, Mr. Scrooge?"

"Bring me the Fleming account, and be quick about it." The old man returned his attentions to some papers on his desk, ignoring the young couple standing, having never been offered seats, before him.

"Extraordinarily chilly, for this time of year," offered the pleasant-looking young man, nervously.

"It'll be chillier if you have to live outdoors," Scrooge countered without looking up. The young man gave up and waited in silence, while his pretty young wife, obviously with child, bit her lower lip, which had begun to tremble.

Robert Cratchit, Scrooge's drab, frayed, pasty, middle-aged, underpaid clerk, brought the requested files, and vanished gratefully into his office.

"Never liked him much," Marley said to his companion, as they watched unseen from a corner of the room. "Jellyfish. No backbone. Works cheap, though."

Scrooge examined the file and grunted. "Mm. Just as I thought. Your note comes due next week ... "

"That's why we're here. If you'll only allow me to explain ... "

"There's nothing to explain. Your house is forfeit, should the loan not be paid in full at the appointed time."

The young man gasped. "Mr. Scrooge, I pray that will not be ... "

"So do I. I've no use for it. Don't need another house.

I suppose I'll just let it out, or sell it to the highest bidder."

"Well, you see, there's been some trouble. Some money I was expecting has been delayed, and there have been some unforeseen expenses with my dear wife Clare's blessed situation ... "

"Your point being?"

"We must rely on your kindness, for we may not be able to redeem the note in time."

"Well, I'm sorry for you, and I pity your poor wife, but there's nothing for me to do."

"We thought perhaps an extension of some kind might be possible ... "

"My dear sir, this is not a charitable institution. I loan money. If people can't repay it, that's not my concern. I must protect my interests." He called to his clerk. "Cratchit, come here and assist this young lady. Good day."

Bob Cratchit helped the young man to carry his wife, who had become faint during the interview, to a chair in the outer office. After a little while, she felt able to walk again, and the young couple left.

"Wretched old scab," said the bogle. "What's he going to do with their money? He made that poor lady cry." With that the little man set about splaying the points on all of Scrooge's quill-pens, and tracking inkblots on several important-looking documents.

"It's only business," said Marley. "It's what I would have done."

"I don't doubt that," countered the bogle.

"Put this in accounts receivable, Cratchit," said Scrooge, returning the file to his clerk.

"Yes, sir."

"Poor Cratchit," said Marley to his companion. "Looking quite the worse for wear. I don't remember all that gray."

"Look at the calendar. Been seven years, old crumb-pot."

"Seven years?"

"This very night."

"But I've only just … "

"Told you, time ain't the same where we've come from."

"My. This very night?"

"Um-hmm. Twenty-fourth of December."

"Hmm."

~

The two of them watched the usual order-of-business at Scrooge & Marley's for the twenty-fourth of December. Beggars and carolers were chased away from Scrooge's door with threats of physical harm and prison sentences. Solicitors for the poor exited no richer than they had entered and were forced to endure the yearly lecture on economics, prisons, workhouses, and the surplus population. Scrooge's nephew, Fred, came in—"Merry

Christmas, Uncle!"—already aglow with Christmas cheer,
and issued his yearly invitation to Christmas dinner, and
received his yearly curse and "Bah, humbug!"

But these appeals for charity and generosity of spirit did not fall entirely on deaf ears. Oh, Scrooge didn't
hear them; he was thoroughly inoculated against their
effect. But Marley's new circumstances made him hear
things with new ears, as it were, especially Scrooge's
nephew's ringing speech on men and women 'opening
their shut-up hearts freely,' and thinking of the people
around them as 'fellow-passengers to the grave.'

"The boy has a point," said Marley, grudgingly
(wishing a little, that he had paid better attention when
he had heard this speech, years before.)

"You should know," said his companion.

～

Finally it was six o'clock. Marley and the bogle
watched as Cratchit helped his employer into his over-
coat. "You'll be wanting the whole day, tomorrow, I suppose?" said the old man to his clerk.

"If it's quite convenient, sir."

"It's not convenient, and it's not fair," Scrooge
sighed. "But I've no objection to your taking work
home with you. I shall expect the Davies contracts, the
McCabe leases, and the Smith-Scott memoranda on my

desk first thing in the morning on the twenty-sixth—in duplicate, of course."

"Of course, sir, thank you, sir," said Cratchit weakly.

"Don't mention it. I'm all heart, I know."

"Yes, sir. Merry Christma ... "

But Scrooge had already left the office, leaving Cratchit to lock up.

~

"Well, this is hopeless," said Marley. "Let's go back to hell. Eternity's a long time, best get started."

"Oh, don't give up so easily," said his miniature, as the two of them watched Cratchit shut everything down, lock everything up, and finish by making a rude gesture to Scrooge's portrait on the wall. "You haven't tried anything yet. Still, it does look pretty bad, I'm afraid. The man seems to be completely lacking in any sort of Christmas *spirit*. But you mustn't let your *spirits* droop. I'm sure it's just a matter of making a *spirited* effort. A bit of the old school *spirit* is what's required. Mustn't be wanting *spirit*, at this time. You know, my throat's a bit parched, I could do with some ... "

"I could use a drink myself. Wait!" Marley froze. "I have it!"

The little man cocked an eyebrow. "Mmm yesss?"

Marley turned to his companion. "What exactly

can we do? We spirits? I mean here, on earth? I know we can get around, unseen, walk through things, and all that—but can we do anything else?"

"I thought you'd never ask," said the bogle. "Come here."

~

"So we can alter our appearance?" said Marley, after a little while.

"That's the least of it. Transubstantiation, instantaneous relocation, acceleration, reversal, and stoppage of time—really, when you're 'on official business,' your powers can be ... "

"Perhaps we can scare some sense into the old crocodile. Perhaps a ghostly visitation. Something really frightening. How's this?" Marley was suddenly covered in a long white sheet, with two eye holes cut out of it. "Oooooo. Repent, Scrooge."

"I don't think that's going to do it."

"Oh, I think it will. I think you'll be surprised. Let's try it."

"I wouldn't, if I were you. You're liable to get thrown out with tomorrow's laundry."

The sheeted spectre drooped. "Well, if you're so smart, what would you do?"

"Well, it's not really up to me, but I think you're

pretty scary as it is."

"Thank you." Marley blinked back into his former shape. "You mean like this?"

"Well, I think you can tart it up a bit. You have been dead for seven years."

"Hmm. Seven years. Yes." Marley rotted before his companion's eyes.

"Ooo, that's good. Now gibber a bit."

～

Scrooge was uneasy. All day he had had a feeling he was being watched. And now, on his way home, the darkness, the cold, and the fog all seemed to conspire together to trip him up, to confuse him, and to rattle his nerves. Twice he heard his name called behind him and turned to see nothing but an empty street, dimly lit by flickering lamplight. As he walked faster, the clatter of his feet on the cobblestones echoed, as if he were being followed. He whirled around and raised his cane. "Who's there?" But of course, no one was there—only the ghost of a mocking laugh, whispered, not quite there, then not there at all, just the fog. The old man shuddered, and hurried on as fast as he could towards home and safety.

He turned at his door for one last look behind him, and grunted his satisfaction. There was no one poised under the street lamp, no one hiding in the dark courtyard. He was alone. With a sigh of relief, he pulled his great ring of keys from its place within his coat, and turned towards his door, at long last, safe.

"Scrooooge … " said his knocker, now a ghastly, glowing image of his dead partner's face. Scrooge leapt back from the door in horror. Marley's face looked him in the eye, grinned, and waggled its tongue horribly at him, before having the good grace to turn back into a knocker.

Scrooge leaned against the wall, his heart hammering. He collected himself, for a moment, then fumbled in the dark for his keys, mumbling to himself about never having dinner in that tavern again and considering the possibility of a lawsuit. But when he opened his door, he opened it with caution and looked behind it before he stepped inside.

Scrooge made his home in his dead partner's house. Usually this didn't bother him; Scrooge was nothing if not a practical man, generally insensible to imaginings and noises in the dark. But as he lit the candle to light his way to his room, he was suddenly aware of what a large, dark, spooky old place it was he lived in. His candle didn't seem to light much of it, and what was lit danced with grotesque shadows that moved somewhat more than they should have. "Humbug," he growled. But he made his way pretty quickly up the stairs and into his room, and locked and double-locked the door behind him.

"Not bad," said the bogle admiringly. "I thought the green glow a particularly nice touch."

"Thanks," said Marley. "This is kind of fun. What next?"

"Use your imagination, you're doing fine. If you need me, I'll be right here." said the little man, nesting inside Marley's right ear. "Eugh. We have *got* to have that talk about hygiene."

～

Chains. The sound of chains being dragged up the worn wooden steps from the cellar. The sound of a slow, heavy, weary tread in the dark, empty hallway on the first floor, each step accompanied by the sound of chains, clanking chains. Then up the stairs, one at a time: one foot, other foot, one foot, other foot; chains dragging rattle and clank up the old stairway to Scrooge's bedroom. Louder, CLANK, and louder, *CLANK*. Deafening echoes filling the halls, the rooms, the rafters of Scrooge's old house, coming closer and closer to his door, until all stops, silent.

Then, BOOM, BOOM, BOOM, thunderous pounding on the locked door.

"Scrooooge." A death-rattle, whispered outside Scrooge's door. Then CRASH! The door thrown open, locks shattered, wood splintered, and inside the door, inside the room with a terrible howl, the fearful, hideous, green-glowing figure of *MARLEY'S GHOST!*

~

Empty. The room was empty. For a moment Marley wondered if he could have made a mistake, somehow gotten the wrong room. It was dark, after all. Then the door flew shut behind him.

"EEEYAAA!" Scrooge sprang from behind it, brandishing a poker over his head. The poker passed through Marley, of course, crashing to the floor beneath him, and the lack of the expected resistance threw old Scrooge off-balance. Before he could regain his equilibrium, Marley floated out of range and turned. The two old men stood still, frozen for a moment, facing each other.

"What do you want with me?" demanded Scrooge, cold and hard as stone.

"Much," replied the other, his words echoing weirdly in the room.

"Ooo. Reverb. Nice," said the bogle.

Then Scrooge charged again, screaming, and swinging the poker wildly. It slashed through Marley again and again, having no more effect than it would have had on smoke. Marley stood his ground and laughed a hollow, ghostly laugh. Finally exhausted,

Scrooge collapsed to his knees and, breathing hard, cast the poker aside. "Who are you, then?"

"Ask me who I was."

"Very well, who were you, then?" snapped the old man.

"In life I was your partner, Jacob Marley."

Scrooge considered this. Then he got up, dusting his hands and knees. "Can you ... can you sit down?"

"I can."

"Well, do it then."

Marley took a seat by the meager fire, his customary seat, the good one, of course; Scrooge took the other. Nothing was said for a while. For a while the two old men just sat in silence, glowering at each other across the fire; for Scrooge and Marley had never been friends. Instead, they were partners. Commodity had made them associates, not affection; years of mistrust and resentment had bonded them together as strong as iron, stronger than friendship or fondness ever could have done. But there was no love lost between them, for there was never any love to begin with; only mutual interest had held them together, and their association had ended at the doors of their counting house.

So they sat staring at each other, in silence. The only sound was the cracking and popping of Scrooge's alleged fire, the creaks and groans of the old house around them, and the sound of the wind, rattling at the windows and wailing around the corners and down the street. Scrooge noticed that his uninvited guest was not really seated on his chair, but was actually floating an inch or two above the chair. Scrooge found this disquieting.

After an excruciating length of time, Marley broke the silence. "How's business?"

Scrooge paused before answering. "Fine. As well as could be expected." Pause. "Got a new safe."

Pause. "New clients? New accounts?"

"Some. It goes. Seven years."

Pause. "Ah."

Pause. "And you?"

Marley was silent in response, but his eyes burned redly for a moment, like banked fires. This sent the chills up and down Scrooge's spine. Marley watched the old man in silence for a while, then said: "You don't believe in me."

"I don't," Scrooge answered, unconvincingly.

"Why do you doubt your senses?"

"Any little thing affects them. Undigested bit of beef, fragment of an underdone potato, et cetera, et cetera. Humbug, that's what you are—a humbug."

With a terrible wail, Marley rose from his chair, literally rose from it, and floated hideously in the air above Scrooge, clanking his chains and howling. As the old man shrank gasping into his chair, Marley floated down until his face was inches away from Scrooge's. Then he peeled his flesh off his skull like a banana and howled at the old man. The old man howled back, terrified.

"Man of the worldly mind, do you believe in me or not?"

"I do, I do, I do. I must!"

"Good."

"Sit down, then!"

"Very well." Marley put his face back on as calmly as if he were adjusting his glasses, and floated back to the chair.

"Careful, he's old!" said the bogle, from inside Marley's ear. "It won't do you any good if you kill him!"

"Be still. I know what I'm doing," thought Marley in reply.

The old man and the ghost of his partner were silent again for a while, two silent figures in the firelight.

"Can you—can you drink something?"

"I believe so."

"Well, then." Scrooge went to get the bottle he kept beside his bed for medicinal purposes, and poured them both a couple of fingers of, it goes without saying, cheap whiskey. "Don't get much company here; certainly not many gh ... of your kind. To your health, if it's not inappropriate, considering the circumstances." Scrooge tossed the liquor down, and hurriedly poured himself another.

Marley raised the glass to his lips; the liquor felt cool to the touch; and it poured straight through him to the cushion of the chair below. Scrooge found this most unpleasant. To change the subject, he pointed to Marley's chains. "You are fettered. Why?"

"Oo—here's your opportunity!" said the bogle. "Lay it on!"

"I wear the chains I forged in life," said Marley, hollowly repeating the record-keeper's words. "I made them link by link, yard by yard, cash box by cash box. Is their pattern strange to you? Or would you know the weight of the chain you bear yourself? It was as heavy and as long as this seven Christmases ago, and you have labored on it since."

This had the desired effect. Scrooge involuntarily looked behind him, half expecting to see several furlongs of ironwork. The bogle chuckled inside Marley's ear.

"So why do you trouble me?" whined Scrooge. "I'm sure you didn't just drop by to be sociable."

Marley improvised wildly, drawing on the themes introduced by Scrooge's nephew. "It is ... um ... required of every man, that the ... uh ... spirit within him should walk abroad among his fellow men, and travel far and wide; and if that spirit goes not forth in life, it is condemned to do so after death. It is doomed to wander through the world—oh, woe is me!—and witness what it cannot share, but might have shared on earth and turned to happiness!"

"'Oh, woe is me?'" said the bogle. "Bit hammy, don't you think?"

"Silence, insect!"

Scrooge grunted skeptically. "Um-hm. So what do you want from me?"

"I've come to warn you."

"Warn me? That's good of you. Warn me of what?"

"Ebenezer Scrooge, I've come to warn you that you must change."

Scrooge had been a businessman too long not to sense a trap when he heard one, and took a long time to answer. "Change, eh? Change what?"

"Almost home, now!" the bogle crowed.

"You must have a Complete and Willing Change of Heart, Ebenezer Scrooge."

"I must, must I?"

"You must."

"And that's what you came here to say?"

"Yes."

"I see. Well. Good enough. Thank you. Consider it changed." Scrooge walked over to his bed, turned down the covers, and turned to Marley, expectantly. "Evening."

"But, I ... "

"I'm most obliged to you. Thank you kindly. Goodnight." Scrooge stood waiting for Marley to leave. "Don't let me keep you."

Marley was nonplussed. He knew he had lost, and he didn't know why. "What shall I do?" he whispered to the bogle.

"I don't know—stall!"

Marley rose into the air once more, wailing and rattling his chains horribly.

"Yes, yes, mind the chandelier—if you're going to keep on with that, take it down the hall, would you? I get very irritable if I don't get a good night's sleep."

"Hear me, Scrooge!" Marley became a literal nightmare, a ghastly skeleton horse with bat wings and blazing eyes, rearing, tearing the air above Scrooge with its terrible hooves.

"Now see here: Stop that! If you want to do that sort of thing, there's a stable down the street! I won't have you flapping about in here, ruining my sleep! You've delivered your message; now begone!"

In desperation, Marley became the Mouth of Hell, as in the old plays—huge and terrifying, a fanged, slavering, stinking mouth for devouring souls; a chorus of the damned singing Gounod filled the air. "Repent, Scrooge!"

Scrooge crossed his arms. "That's enough." Scrooge quietly walked over to where Marley hung. "Put out those flames and quit slobbering on my carpet. Come down here." Marley turned back into himself, more or less, and floated down. "Now, what do you really want?"

"I'm here to make you see the error of your ways."

"The error of my ways." Scrooge grunted, nodded, and walked away a bit. Then he turned and fixed Marley with a flashing eye. "What's wrong with 'em?"

"Well, uh ... you're, uh ... "

"I'm cheap, I'm tight. I'm not 'nice.' Anything else?"

"Well, really, you ... "

"Hypocrite. Dare to waltz in here gauded up like some damn Christmas tree and tell me to change my life? There's nothin' wrong with it. I pay my taxes. I obey the law. I'm good at my work. I make money. I'm a damned good businessman, and that's all that's required of me."

"Shouldn't mankind be your business?" Marley offered weakly.

Scrooge spat into the fire. "Old maid. Point your finger at me! What right have you to tell me to change my life? What do you want me to do? Be *pleasant* to people?" Scrooge simpered and did a ghastly mockery of a smile. "Be *generous*?" He skipped about, tossing imaginary coins in the air. "Reward fools? Subsidize people too stupid, too lazy to work, too lazy to get a proper job?" Scrooge snorted. "Hypocrite. Come here."

He drew Marley to the window. "Look out there—you see that storm?" They listened to the thunder, so rare in a winter storm, and watched as London began to crystallize under a sheet of ice. "That sleet beating against the windows, that wind howling—for a while, you and I *were* that storm. We rode on top of it, you and I, above the wind, above the fury. Others got wet, others got soaked, others went down beneath the waves, but we survived, you and I, and prospered. And now you tell me that what we did was wrong? Liar."

"You yourself told me, 'We'd best take care of ourselves, Mr. Scrooge. It's a certainty and a fact of this life that no one's going to do it for us.' And for years and years, that's just what we did.

"And now you come to me, tricked up like the ghost in some fourth-rate *Hamlet,* and tell me, with suitably sepulchral tones, to change my life. Well, *you go to hell.* You go straight to hell, Jacob! Or go back to it. Ha! That's a good one! Ha! Go to hell, old ghost! Ha! I laugh in your face!"

Scrooge barked his laugh in Marley's face, and Marley staggered beneath the blow of it as if he had been struck.

"Begone, miserable spirit!" Scrooge laughed again. His contempt hit Marley like a wave, and the ghost of Jacob Marley flickered undecidedly, wavered, disassembled, came back, then—"And shut the door on your way out!" And Marley blinked out and was gone, as if he had never been there.

Scrooge blew out his candle and went to bed.

"Well, that didn't work," said the bogle. Marley and his accomplice were sitting on the edge of the dome of St. Paul's. The storm had cleared, the stars were beginning to peep out, and London once again sparkled under the night sky.

"You were a lot of help," said Marley.

"I couldn't think of anything to say. After all, he has a point."

"Of course he has a point. He's right. Well, we tried."

"That we did, old muffin. Mind, I thought that would do it. Against anyone else, it would have. Thought the Hell-Mouth an especially nice touch."

"Thanks," Marley sighed. He let his chin fall to his chest and a fat, salty tear ploshed onto one of the chains on his wrist.

"Careful, old thing. Won't do any good to rust now, will it?"

"I suppose we have to go back now?"

"Well, you have until cock's crow. Might as well enjoy your last bit of freedom."

"If there were only some way—but what can we do? He's always been like this. The man's totally set in his ways, unmoving, unchangeable. Might as well be talking to a wall."

"Always been this bad, eh?"

"Yes, even when ... " Marley stopped. "Actually, when we first met—hmm." He turned to the bogle. "A

while ago you said that, for us, time was a lot more ... flexible than it is for mortals?"

"Certainly. You can start it up and stop it like a watch, for what that's worth. Why? Do you want to go back and look at your childhood or something?"

"Not exactly ... not mine."

Chapter Four

"**E**xcellent disguise," said the bogle. "He'll never know it's you."

"It is rather cunning, isn't it?" said Marley, turning around. "I think it becomes me, don't you?"

"Don't push it. It's a good disguise."

"Now, how do we do this? How does this work?"

"I don't really know. We've been approved, of course, but how the process works—don't ask me. These time things can be tricky—sometimes they have a mind of their own."

"But we'll be able to take him back?"

"Theoretically; that's how the Past Function functions. But again, I've never used it m'self. We'll see, I suppose."

"And will we be able to get back when we want to?"

"I assume so; but really, what's the difference? You, of all people, have nothing to lose."

The transformed Marley paused. "Indeed. I suppose you're right. Well, we'd best be about it. Wish me luck."

"I do, old pimple, I do. And," he said, settling once again into Marley's ear, "I'll be here if you need me."

"That's a comfort."

~

"Who the hell are you?"

Scrooge was not having a good night. He sat bolt upright in his bed, staring at the new apparition that floated in the air before him. "Get out of my house," he said, his hand inching towards the fireplace.

"Get up, old man, we're going on a little trip."

"I've had quite enough of spirits for the evening, thank you. Come any closer and I'll bean you with this poker."

The spirit lifted its little finger and sent the poker floating back to its resting-place beside Scrooge's tiny fire. Floating above the old man's bed was a ragamuffin street-rat, a cockney boy about eight years old, filthy, tattered, liberally freckled, and missing a tooth. A shock of red hair hung down over one eye, and his grin was irresistible.

Scrooge resisted. "Who are you?"

The little spirit spread his arms and announced proudly, "I'm the Ghost of Christmas Past, guv'nor."

The old man snorted. "Long past?"

"No, *your* past, you old fart!"

Scrooge leapt to his feet, and started looking for something to throw. "Cheeky little imp!" Finding nothing he wanted to risk, he said, "What the devil brings you here?"

"Your welfare."

"My welfare, is it? Thank you for your concern. I am so obliged." He began to climb back into bed. "I think an unbroken night of rest and quiet would be ... "

"Your reclamation, then." The boy's voice rang out with surprising authority, and the covers flew out of the old man's hand. "Rise, and walk with me," he said, holding out his hand.

"'Rise, and walk with me?'" said the bogle, from within Marley/Christmas Past's ear. "Where did that come from?"

"I haven't the slightest!" thought Marley in reply. "Must be part of the arrangement."

"Well, keep it up! It's good!"

"Rise?" said Scrooge. "But Spirit, I am a mortal ... "

"That's *your* lookout, guv'nor! Hold on!" and the boy grasped the old man's hand and lifted. Scrooge, wailing his protest and his underdress, his vertigo and his lumbago, rose into the air and floated several feet above his bed. "I'll fall! Where are you taking me? It's winter—I'll catch my death!" Unheeding, the young spirit led him to the window, opened it with a grand gesture, and together they sailed through the window and out into the night sky.

The sky all around them was brilliant as a jeweller's shop, and filled with song, every star singing with all its might, old constellations and newborn, each star competing for glory; the sweep of the stars, an exaltation against the dark. "Look around you!" cried the boy. He threw back his head and laughed and whooped as they sailed through the sky.

At first, Scrooge was breathless, paralyzed with fear, his heart hammering in his chest. He yelled a long yell that began as terror, stark terror, at seeing London stretched below him, far, far below him; then it became a demand ("I demand that you put me down!") and then a plea ("Please put me down?") and then the yell turned to crabby outrage, as Scrooge felt more and more himself. Finally, as the ragamuffin whipped him through cartwheels and loop-the-loops and barrel-rolls and great dives, the old man's yell became—wonder of wonders— a giggle, then a laugh, then a great, whooping laugh, and then a great "Wheeeeeeeeee!" that pealed and echoed and soared along with them through the star-bespangled sky.

"Where do you take me, spirit?"

"You tell me, for you direct our journeys by your memories, and the love therein."

"Well, you're just full of surprises, aren't you?" said the bogle.

"It isn't me, I tell you!" thought Marley.

"Then best just relax and enjoy the ride!"

So they did. And the stars began to whirl around them, to cluster and to blow like snowflakes in the wind, whirling, all around them, whirling snowflakes, whirling snow ...

A bright winter's morning in the country—blinding white, the air like liquid crystal, glistening birdsong, every branch and bush and fencepost and wagon-rut sparkling with a thousand, thousand diamonds.

"Do you know this place?" asked the disguised Marley.

"Know it?" cried Scrooge. "I was a boy here!"

It was an old, country boarding-school, not of the first class, or even the second, but full of noise and good cheer, nonetheless, for the boys were hooting and laughing and shouting their good-byes as they scrambled to leave for their Christmas holiday. Scrooge knew every one by name, and called to each with a nickname, or a joke, or a "remember when ... ?" But the boys went on, not heeding the old spectre in their midst.

"Spirit, they don't answer me," said the old man. "Can't they hear? Or are these but the shadows of things that have been?"

"No, guv'nor," the ragamuffin answered, "these

things is real. As real as could be. You and me is the shadows, guv'nor."

The school emptied out and soon every boy was gone, save one. From their vantage point inside Christmas Past, Marley and the bogle watched old Scrooge as he remembered.

"Hmm," thought Marley to the bogle. "Look at that."

"What?"

"Look at his eyes," thought Marley. "Never thought to see—hmm."

Old Scrooge stood in a corner, watching the sad little boy wander, alone and forgotten, through the empty school rooms. "Poor boy," said the old man to himself, unaware of the single tear that was making its way down through the crags and crevices of his face. Of course, the boy he was watching was himself.

Again, swirling snowflakes obscured the scene, and then:

⁓

"Papa? Papa?" said another little boy, timidly pushing open the great door to his father's study, a dim, brown, cave-like room smelling of books and leather.

"What the hell is this?" cried Marley, alarmed.

"Something the matter, old bean?"

"Papa? Papa, are you there?"

"This—this isn't Scrooge's past ... "

"What do you want?" a gruff voice mumbled thickly. A man sat at the only table in the room. His face was in darkness, the low-hanging light illuminating only the glass in his hand, and the half-empty bottle beside it.

"Mother wants you, Papa. She called for you."

"Go 'way." The figure turned away from him, poured another glass.

"But she's sick again, Papa, and she told me—"

"Get out, I said!" The figure stood, suddenly huge and dark against the light, and picked up the little boy under the arms, and threw him into the hall, thundering the door shut behind him. The boy, dazed and hurt, stifled his sobs. Behind him he heard the lock shot, hard.

"Well, I'm not sure I understand," said the bogle. "If this isn't Scrooge's past, whose is it?"

"It's mine!" cried Marley in horror.

~

"How did this happen?" said Marley, furiously turning on his companion. "We're supposed to be visiting Scrooge's past, not mine!"

"Don't know," said the bogle, a little too innocent-ly. "Really, I'm quite as surprised as you are."

Marley's eyes narrowed with fury. "You tricked me! You knew about—well, I won't put up with it! If you think I'm going to go through all this again ... How do we get out of here?"

"I don't think we can, old bean," said the little man. "I think once you start this thing, you just have to ride it till the end. I think you're stuck."

"Well, I won't do it," said Marley. He waved a hand and suddenly the scene before them froze.

"What did you do?" demanded the bogle. In front of them, the weeping boy had become a statue, frozen, immobile, one tear suspended midair, floating above the floor.

"You said we could stop time," said Marley. "Well, I just did."

"You can't do this!"

"Watch me."

"Marvelous." The bogle crossed his arms and floated in front of Marley's face, like a tiny fury. "Well, I hope you like the view."

"I like it just fine."

"Good. You're going to be looking at it for a long time. Novel way to spend eternity. A trifle dull, though."

"You mean ... ?"

"Of course! What did you think? We're stuck here, too!"

"Forever? Just this?"

The bogle just looked at him, arms crossed, tapping a tiny foot.

"Oh, hell," said Marley, miserably. Time started up again, and the boy's tear splashed onto the floor. Marley sighed. "It was bad enough the first time."

~

"Fan!" cried Scrooge, watching another scene from his past. "Sweet Fan, alive again!" The hard lines of his face softened as he watched his little sister come into the schoolroom, and embrace another Scrooge, now a young man.

"Oh, Ebenezer! Father is so much kinder than he used to be ... "

And as Scrooge, entranced, watched his younger self and his sister—"She had a large heart, spirit!"— Marley was again whirled back through the snows into his own past. He watched, grief-stricken, as:

~

"Mama! Mama!" cried the little boy, sobbing, red, his face streaked with crying. But the tall, silent men carried her off, carried her away from him. No one explained to him why she didn't wake up, or smile, or speak to him any longer; but he knew. "Mama!"

"Well, boy, what do you want?" Another memory overlapped: his father's voice, rusty and unused, as he sat in the darkened room. "What do you ... " A long pause, with just the man's eyes burning in the darkness, then: "Come here."

The boy froze in the doorway.

"Come here, damn you!"

And the boy crept into the room a step at a time, into the room where his father sat in the dark and drank. He walked as if at any second the floor before him would suddenly gape open and hurl him into bottomless darkness. His father—"Closer!"—held his shoulders and looked him in the eyes, searching his face. Then the man crumpled and clutched the terrified boy to him; hot, wet, making little coughing sounds and holding him too tight; after a while he grew quiet and pushed the boy away and mumbled something; then his head dropped to the table, and he was still. The boy waited and waited in silence, trembling; then he left the room as quietly as a shadow and ran upstairs and lay on his bed all night in his clothes, eyes wide open, listening, afraid.

Then: having to dress in clothes that were too tight, in shoes that hurt his feet, and walk, stumbling, dragged beside his father—"Keep up, damn you!"—

behind the black carriage with the box in it. People's faces, staring, hats off; his father's face, set like stone, walking behind the carriage and the box. Then the rain, and watching, as they put the box into the hole in the ground, and the hollow sound of the dirt, shoveled on top of it. And walking, with his father, silently, home, his father's hand hurting, crushing his small one like a vise.

And shortly after that, being sent away.

~

"Must we?" Marley gasped, ashen.

The little spirit floated before his face and looked him in the eye, serious for once. "I know it hurts, old thing. But there's nothing to be done for it."

"Please—can't we go back to hell? That wasn't as bad as this."

The little spirit shook its head, and flew down to pat his hand with a tiny hand. "There, there, old thing. There, there."

~

So as Scrooge, lost in the world of his own memories, watched scene after scene from his past, sometimes rapt, at times laughing, dancing once, and once begging someone not to go, Marley and his spirit companion saw scenes that Scrooge didn't see—other, grimmer scenes that burned like a brand.

Marley sadly watched as the silent little boy he had once been was sold into apprenticeship at the old man's warehouse. The boy was friendless save for the old man's occasional, harried kindness—"Mr. Marley! Not so glum, if you please! What will you take for a smile, sir? A toffee? Two? You drive a hard bargain, sir!"—sleeping under the counter, and living in terror of the bullying, the hissed threats, the mean tricks and cruel pinches of the older apprentice, Dick Wilkins—"Give me that! And you know what you'll get if you tell!"

The years went by, marked only by the old man's annual party—"Yo, ho, my boys! No more work! It's Christmas, Dick! Christmas, Mr. Marley!"—and dance. After several years of silent watching, the boy had finally worked up the stammering courage to ask the youngest of the Fezziwig girls to dance. She giggled and blushed and, looking at the floor, agreed. He took her moist hand into his dry one and led her into the dance, and all was going surprisingly well until Dick Wilkins stuck out his foot and tripped him, sending Marley sprawling into the thick of the dancers.

The music stopped. "Ho, Mr. Marley! My word, sir!" laughed the old man, helping the crimson-faced boy to his feet. "No more punch for you!" Everyone else laughed, too, particularly Dick Wilkins, as the boy, his face ablaze, retreated into the shadows. Farther and farther into the shadows he shrank, away from the music, away from the laughter, until he was alone, no longer obliged to smile and nod. He stood alone in the shadows, his eyes burning. If anyone had glanced his way, they might have been startled at the wolfish expression on the young man's face—how hungry he looked, in the shadows, alone.

"I saw what Wilkins did," said a voice. Young Marley, startled, turned to see the new boy—Scrooge, wasn't it?—standing beside him. The boy was lean as a whippet and twice as sharp, with a gleam in his eyes not unlike his own. "I know how we can get even," said the boy; and with these words the partnership of Scrooge and Marley was born.

～

Marley watched the history of their lives unfolding before him like some blighted gray flower. He saw how they had grown together in secrets and whispers and shared confidences—Scrooge and Marley, always off in a corner whispering together. He saw how together they planned revenge for the injustices of the world. "It's an unfair world, Mr. Marley, and that's how it is; but seeing as that's how it is, maybe we can work that to our advantage. I am determined to be the one that's stepping on and not the one getting stepped."

So the two boys worked harder and longer than any of the others. Mr. Fezziwig soon noticed Marley's cleverness, and put him to school on the books and the accounting; Mr. Scrooge was always the front man—"Can I get that for you, ma'am? Yes sir, thank you sir, only too kind, sir"—smiling all the while, and all the while watching, and biding his time. As they grew older, they were running the business, so good were they at it, and Fezziwig trusted them so.

Of course they had their revenge on Dick Wilkins. Wilkins, like most bullies, had grown before the rest of the boys and then had stopped growing in any way at all. To tell the truth, he was a little slow, and eventually, all he was fit for in the warehouse was hauling the heavier items, barrels and sacks of feed, a job he did without complaint, like an old dray horse accustomed to its labor. So when he was called to the office of the two young managers, he had no inkling—"I'm afraid we've no further use for your services, Wilkins," said Scrooge with a smile. "Collect your severance, and be kind enough to be clear of the place by closing, won't you?" Wilkins bobbed his head and left the room, and Scrooge and Marley fell cackling into each others' arms.

Marley saw then, from his new perspective, something he hadn't seen before: Even with the door closed,

Wilkins had heard the two laughing at him. His face reddened and he looked confused for a moment, and then he went to ask one of the boys what a "severance" was. After the boy had sympathetically explained it to him, the man's eyes welled up as he tried to think what he was going to do now, and where he was going to go.

"Proud of yourself?" asked the bogle.
"Not especially," answered Marley.

Time passed, and eventually Fezziwig took them on as partners, which was his doom—for their influence and their contacts spread throughout the company, eventually devouring it and forcing the old man into an early retirement in a cottage by the sea with his good wife. He died shortly after; his work was his life, and deprived of that, he didn't know what else to do with himself, so he died.

"Didn't know that, either."
"Didn't know, or didn't care?"

Marley watched grimly as his life spun out before him. The firm became Scrooge and Marley, Fezziwig no more. No more dances were held in the warehouse, no more Christmas parties. The warehouse and the counting house became places of business: sober, somber, and respectable. As for the two new owners, Marley watched them go out into the world like a pair of ravening wolves—not rushing among the sheep, biting, scattering, and panicking them, but watching from the hill, until a sheep became weak or sick or old or especially fat; and then descending to feed.

But within the law, always within the law. They were nothing if not scrupulous; everything was done to the letter of the law—for the law is there to protect scoundrels, too, and they knew it. They would never have drawn the law's wrath down upon them—the law was their friend. Many a time, against the protests of some abused and misled dupe, their answer would be a shrugged, helpless, "It's the law."

So they grew fat on the innocent, and grew rich on the gullible and the trusting. And because they trusted no one, they trusted each other not at all— each suspected the other of lining his pockets at his expense; each was sure the other was cheating him, as he was cheating the other; and they stole from each other, convinced they were being stolen from.

And always within the law; always within the law.

Marley couldn't look away, as much as he would have liked to. He saw himself and his partner grow old together—old in their mistrust, their suspicion, their kept and whispered secrets, and in their minute and exacting division of the spoils.

And when the end came, Marley watched very intently indeed, as:

Scrooge made his move to take over the business. When Marley had found out, he confronted Scrooge with the misdeed. The old man smiled a yellow-toothed smile and said that it was none of his business, or rather, none of his business, anymore. Marley picked up a ruler, and, in a spasm of fury, raised it. Then the side of his mouth went funny all of a sudden, and he seemed to forget what he was doing. He dropped the ruler and wandered back into his office, where he sat at his desk for a long time, till closing time, barely moving, just rocking a little, and staring at a spot on the wall where nothing was. When six o'clock came, he went to the safe; walking oddly, with hitches and jerks, like a battered wind-up toy. He took one of the cash boxes out of the safe, and picked up the coins in his hands and let them run through his fingers like water, just looking at them with glassy eyes and an odd fix to his jaw. Then he jammed as many coins as he could carry into his hands and his pockets, and, still jerking along like a broken machine, walked out of the counting-house door leaving a trail of fallen money behind him.

There was a raised stone platform at the end of the street where politicians used to stand to give speeches. Marley hitched himself up the steps to the platform, eyes fixed, jaws clenched in a terrible rictus grin. When he reached the top, he began to whirl like a shattered doll, hurling the money away from him angrily, furiously, making odd choking sounds in the back of his throat. The coins pelted away from him in vicious handfuls, a barrage, a fountain of copper, silver, and gold. Marley whirled, hurtling the coins away from him as hard as he could, barking savagely to the sky above him, "No good! No good! None! None! None! None! None!" Then he pulled more coins out of his pockets and crammed them into his mouth, gagging on them and spewing them out again, spilling wet mouthfuls of them onto the stones.

Scrooge watched horrified from the door of the counting house, then called a constable. He, the constable, and Cratchit subdued Marley, who was now looking at his twisted old hands and saying, "Nothing left. Empty. Never was ... " His mouth moved silently for a moment, and then he whispered, "Gone." Cratchit walked him home, for he couldn't remember where it was, and put him to bed, from which he never arose; while Scrooge spent the rest of the evening scouring the cobblestones for coins that the children had missed—not too proud to crawl, not caring that people laughed at him, the old man scrabbled in the dark on his hands and knees for a few coins. He found a couple, and pocketed them.

When last they saw each other, Scrooge had been called to the deathbed by Marley's housekeeper. He

stood silently in the door of the bedroom, watching as his former partner struggled to breathe his last. At one point, Marley opened his eyes and stared at him— seemed to know him, recognized him, surely—but said nothing, only glared at him accusingly. Scrooge looked right back, bold as brass, and watched as the last choking gasping came and Marley's breath was finally stopped. Then he put on his hat and gloves (for he had never removed his coat) and went out and had his dinner.

~

"You remember it now?" asked the bogle.

Marley didn't move. He was shattered, aghast, shaken to the roots of his soul. He had seen the sum of his life in a few moments, every grasping, clutching bit of it; and he was rocked by its poverty and its waste. Now he could only look down at his empty hands, in their chains—hands that had spent every waking moment scrabbling and clawing for gain, for gold, only to find out, too late, like the man in the fairy tale, that all he held was a handful of dead leaves.

"I deserve these," he said, running his chains through his fingers. The bogle nodded.

Then his hands clenched and Marley turned white-hot with fury. "And Scrooge! That wretch! He did this to me! Well, *he* can go to hell, now!" he raged. "He can join me, he can rot in hell beside me for all eternity—I'll be damned if I'll lift my littlest fingernail to save him! I'll be damned if I will!"

Marley stopped then, and was silent for a while.

"Rather, old thing," said the bogle gently, "you'll be damned if you don't."

Marley turned his back on the little man. The bogle flew around him, and lit on his shoulder. "Don't damn yourself to spite him, Marley me darlin'. He ain't worth it. He's your one chance to save yourself. Best take it, m'dear."

Marley paused a long time, then bit out through clenched jaws, "No. I'm done with him."

"I understand. Well, perhaps you're right."

~

They re-joined Scrooge, and Marley now fully re-inhabited the boyish, ragamuffin Spirit of Christmas Past. Old Scrooge had been unaware of their parting or their coming back, unaware of anything but the scenes before him. Before him now stood a mature man, no longer quite young, involved in a rather heated discussion with a lady of some beauty. She had removed a ring from her finger and placed it on the open ledger-book on the desk between them.

"Belle!" cried the old man.

She looked at the younger man calmly. "Tell me, Ebenezer, if this had never been between us, would you seek me out and try to win me now? You, who measure everything by gain?"

"Yes! Yes, I would! Oh, yes! Belle, don't ... " said the old man, arguing desperately.

"You think not," said his younger self, though no one would have been convinced by the way he said it.

She smiled at him then, and wiped the tears from her eyes. "I release you," she said. "With a full heart, for the love of him you once were: May you be happy in the life you have chosen." She raised her hand, and put it to his cheek and let it rest there, for a moment, as she looked into his eyes for the last time.

"Belle, don't go! Don't go! Please, please don't go!" pleaded old Scrooge, on his knees now, his hands clasped before him, begging her. He clutched at the hem of her skirt, trying to stop her.

To no effect. The fabric passed through his knotted old fingers like air, as she crossed to the door of the office, and opened it.

"Belle!" a terrible, heart-broken wail from the old man.

She paused at the door and turned a little, as if she had heard someone calling her name from a great distance. Then she left, and the door closed behind her, its bell tinkling cheerily. The younger Scrooge pocketed the ring and went back to work with a barely voiced sigh of relief; while the old man he was to become lay on the office floor and wept. He wept, for the last hope of any love in his life had just gone out the door, and he knew it. He wept, for he knew the years before him would be empty, ash-filled, lifeless dust, the last bit of life, of love, of hope having left him forever. He wept for the young man too blind to see the end of his life as he stood in it.

"Go after her," he pleaded, but the young man couldn't hear, and went on about his accounts.

The scene faded, leaving him alone with the boy-spirit of Christmas Past. "Why do you delight to torture me?" Scrooge choked out.

"These are but the shadows of things that have been," said the Marley/spirit coldly. "That they are what they are—do not blame me."

"Show me no more!" cried the old man. "I cannot bear it."

"Very well." And they were back in Scrooge's bedroom. The old man sat weeping in his chair, his hands covering his face. Marley and the bogle watched a moment, invisible.

Then the bogle charged the weeping Scrooge's head like a hornet, taunting him and laughing viciously. "That's it, old fool! Cry! Louder! Louder! How does it feel? Maybe you should have … "

"What are you doing?" said Marley, shocked.

"He deserves what he's got," cried the little spirit, laughing and dive-bombing about the old man's head.

"Yes, but ... "

"Old fool! Old wretch! Should have thought! Should have paid some attention! No use sitting there blubbering now! You've made your empty bed—now you'd best get used to lyin' in it!"

"Stop it," said Marley, quietly.

"What?" The bogle froze.

"Stop it. Leave him alone."

"Why? This is the man who ... "

"I know who it is."

"But he ... "

"I know what he did." A voice like iron. "Leave him be."

The two of them watched the old man weeping in his chair.

"I thought you said you were done with him."

"I am."

They watched a while longer. By the time they had left, old Ebenezer Scrooge had cried himself to sleep.

～

"Why did you stop me?" asked the bogle. The two of them were perched once more on the dome of St. Paul's, high above the city. Below them the city slept, wrapped in silence, and sleepy clock-towers gently chimed the hours 'tween midnight and morning. It was a peaceful and quiet Christmas Eve, Jacob Marley's last Christmas Eve on this earth. "You hate him, don't you, got a right to, after what he did to you. Why'd you stop me?"

"Don't know," said Marley.

"Yes, you do," said the little spirit.

"Can't you leave me in peace for a while?"

"Suppose you're right, as usual. This is, after all, your last look at this city and these stars, now that you've decided to let the old cold-sore rot in his own mess. Not that he doesn't deserve it, of course. He deserves that and a whole lot more. And he'll get it. If you think your chains are heavy, wait till you see what they've got in store for old Scrooge. Once they've got him locked down, he won't look like anything so much as the scrap heap back of a shipping-yard. That pile's going to be about 3 percent Scrooge, and 97 percent old iron."

"Do you mind?" said Marley.

"Mind what, old bean-pot?

"Would you mind plugging up that seemingly endless flow of chat?"

The bogle, surprised and offended, did. For a while the two of them just watched the stars in silence, as they made their solemn rounds above them.

"Shooting star," observed Marley.

The bogle, still smarting, said nothing.

"If you must know," said Marley, "I felt sorry for him."

"Excuse me? Were you addressing me, sir?"

"Oh, stop it. It was just that, bad as he no doubt is, and getting what he no doubt deserves, he just seemed so ... "

"Vulnerable? Unhappy? Disgusting?"

"Human. He seemed so human, then, crying over his lost love and his wasted life. Like all of us, somehow."

"Aren't getting sentimental on me, are you?"

"What you were doing just didn't seem fair."

"I see." The bogle smiled then, a private little smile that Marley didn't see. He waited quite a long time, and then said, "You know, it's a good long while 'til cock's crow."

"Hmm?" Marley grunted.

"The game isn't over yet. The hardest part's done. You've chipped the glacier, broken the shell, made him feel something again, probably for the first time since his voice broke."

"I'm listening."

"He's open, now. To simplify a terrifically complicated metaphysical concept, his heart's open a crack— all you have to do now is put something inside it. A liberal dosage of Christmas cheer, and you're home free, old chap!"

In spite of himself, Marley smiled at the little man. "And I suppose you have some idea of how to do this?"

"Well, yes, um, I do have—but don't worry! It's not like the other."

"That's a relief."

"The other was just activating the basic life-review mechanism. This one is something—or rather, some-one—with a life on their own terms."

"I'm going to be playing another part?"

"Not exactly playing one. More like, living a part."

"How do you mean?"

"Well, 'the Ghost of Christmas Past' was a wonderful idea, a wonderful part, and you played it very, very well, blah, blah, blah. But there really is a Ghost of Christmas Present—or someone very like him."

"I don't like the sound of this."

The little man grinned broadly. "You're over the worst of it, Marley m'dear. This next part is pure pleasure."

Chapter Five

"**R**ise, and walk with me!"

"Not again? Go away," said Scrooge, from beneath his bedclothes.

He had been awake for some time. The visits of the various spirits and the visions of the evening had released a flood of unwelcome memories. He was tortured; his bed had become a rack on which he tossed from one hateful image to another. There was no escaping: His mind was a glass that showed him what he had become with terrible clarity.

So he was grateful for the distraction when he heard the laughter coming from the next room. Scrooge's bedroom adjoined a parlour/sitting room; but as Scrooge never entertained, the room had become over the years an empty, dusty cupboard/lumber room, where Scrooge kept his firewood, broken shovels, old boots, and the like. From the room beyond, came a great, rolling laugh, and a rosy-golden light spilled from beneath the door.

"Come and know me better, man!"

"Fat chance of that," said Scrooge, burrowing further into his bedclothes.

Then there was a sound of music and laughter; and even under his covers Scrooge could tell that his room had been invaded, been filled with light, as if the sun had decided, in the middle of the night, to rise in the old man's bedroom. The light was so strong that it shone right through his several layers of frayed quilts and moth-eaten blankets, making them transparent. Even Scrooge could not ignore a phenomenon like this and, shielding his eyes, he poked his pointy old nose above his blankets.

An immense, shining face filled the room.

Scrooge fainted.

~

"Won't hurt a bit, m'dear," said the bogle.

"Are you sure?" Marley had said, a little frightened. He stood waiting, not sure for what, or for Whom. "Should I—should I do anything?"

"The invitation's been sent. Just be patient. It's all taken care of."

Suddenly Marley felt warm, very warm, inside and out, as if he stood basking before a great fire on a bitter winter night. He heard music, faintly, and was dimly aware, peripherally, of dancing—of celebrants

dancing attendance, leaping, whirling, clanging cymbals and tambours and drums.

Then he felt the closeness of something immense, something huge moving in the air next to him. "What's this?" he cried.

Then the Presence entered him, and he laughed.

He felt the laughter rippling out of him, like a wave released, flowing, blessing everything it touches, healing, and making things grow.

And he saw the effect of the laughter—saw it change and heal the world; not only uplifting to the people it touched, causing them to leave their troubles for a moment, to grow, and to expand beyond them; but the wind, and the grasses, the waters, and the very stars, laughed along with him, and sang their joy.

And others, too—the air around him, the sky above him became filled with faces. spirits. winged and unwinged, beautiful and horned, young and old; and the laughter, like light—like a wave, reached out, and illuminated the faces, till one by one, they laughed, and shone, and were transformed, and uplifted, rising like bubbles through the air, to where?—and one came down before it went wherever it was going, and kissed him on the cheek, and pulled his beard, told him a secret, and laughed, and flew away.

Marley wondered—the joy inside him was stampeding, out of control. He felt like Phaeton, trying to hold the reins of the sun's huge, fiery horses; he felt the light and the power coursing through him, changing him.

"Why didn't I know this? Why wasn't I told?"

"You were, you were," said the stars, blowing great razz-berries at him.

He laughed again. Marley laughed, and the laughter rolled out of him like gentle thunder heralding a warm summer's rain, huge, and blessing, and making things grow. He felt things cracking inside him, and falling, exploding away—old ideas, brittle shells, papier-mâché husks—all too small for him now, now that he knew what he knew.

And he laughed, and laughed.

The little spirit was aghast. "Marley? Are you in there?"

For Marley was transformed now, engulfed by the Presence: His face was as big as the sun, and he stood huge, bearded, and crowned with a holly wreath, cloaked in a long green robe trimmed with white, with a golden light flowing off him like water.

The Marley/Spirit of Christmas Present laughed hugely, then gently, and took the little man on his fingertip. "Never felt better, little imp," he said. Then he winked and added, "Really. Never felt better."

"Now, let's see what we can do for—no, *to* that sorry old gas-bag, Scrooge."

And the two went off in a cloud of laughter, trailing laughter behind them like a cloak, and everywhere they touched was blessed.

~

"Wake up, you pathetic old scab," said the Spirit. Scrooge, still passed out on his bed, opened one groggy eye.

"Go away," he said. "Haven't you and your kind done enough to me? Go away and leave me alone."

"Not tonight, Scrooge." The Spirit grinned at him. "You have ignored and reviled me and my kind for too, too many years. It won't work for you this evening. Come."

"Where? Where are we going? I'm not sure I want to ... "

"As if you have a choice," laughed the Spirit, and away they flew.

~

They traveled, then, the four of them, really—Scrooge, tiny and protected in the Spirit's great hand, Marley and the bogle, enfolded in the Spirit's great heart—and again Marley had no say as to where they went, or what they saw, for this Spirit seemed to have his own agenda, his own places to be and things to attend to. They traveled the world that night; and both Scrooge and Marley saw many things they had never seen, or had avoided seeing, or had forgotten that they had seen. They visited rough men who worked in the mines, they saw men at sea, they went to Scrooge's nephew's dinner; and everywhere they went, Marley saw the same thing again and again:

—in two men sharing a half-pint of cheap whiskey and a song, huddled before a tiny fire under their roof for the night, London Bridge;

—in two old women sitting before a fire, laughing together till the tears ran down their faces over the loves of their youth;

—in a pair of lovers whispering their love and fearfully, desperately, gravely, touching each other for the first time or the thousandth;

—in neighbors coming together, helping a woman to bury her husband or her father or her child, weeping with her, sharing her grief and her burden;

—in a man stopping his work, taking a child onto his lap, and teaching the child how to tie a knot or read a word or make something, again and again, until the child proudly accomplished it on his own;

—and in one of the alms-houses, on this night of all nights, the bible-reader leaving off the dour, stern threats and lectures, and instead retelling the poor the story they all knew: how on a certain night (like all nights), a baby was born, and a star heralded its coming, and how mother and child were visited by friends and neighbors, bringing gifts of love and welcome.

The Spirit showed them all this, and more, in their travels that night. And Scrooge learned much; but it was Jacob Marley, within the Spirit, seeing with His eyes and feeling with His heart, who learned the most. For Scrooge was changed by what he saw; but Marley was changed by what he *was*; like a horse, he was ridden, and ridden gratefully; and like a horse, he was led: from some shabby, sad old lean-to of a stable to a palace of gold.

~

Of course they ended up at the Cratchit's. Somehow the Spirit fitted himself into their tiny home as comfortably as the starry sky, and the four of them watched the Cratchits at their meager Christmas dinner. They saw a good deal of loving, teasing, and minor squabbles among the smaller Cratchits, naturally. But what Marley noted most was the constant, hovering concern over the littlest boy; whom everybody watched (but never let him see their concern) so that when he fell into a fit of coughing after a bit of Christmas punch went down the wrong pipe, first they all looked at him in frozen horror, then fell in to universal back-slapping and too-loud joking; then several of the smaller children also feigned to choke and cough, to cheer up the little boy, and make him less self-conscious; and the rest of the family, thinking this was a good idea, sounded for a while like the waiting room at the charity hospital. This made the little boy laugh and they joined him, relieved; but with all the attention and excitement, he was soon tired, and soon he fell asleep on his father's lap.

Then they began to sing, these Cratchits; they sang funny songs and songs of the season. (Scrooge was amazed to discover that his clerk had a sense of humor. Bob did a very comical turn as a young lady who said "No, no, no!" as she got herself farther and farther into trouble. It was so universally popular that he had to do it twice.) When they asked the littlest boy, awake once more, what song he wanted, it was the oldest song they knew, a lullaby for a child. As their voices rose in the ancient "lullay, lullays" Marley heard a whisper: "Behold." He felt a light-headedness, and another shift in his eyes; and what he saw was this: There was a golden cord that bound the family together, heart to heart; literally, a shining cord of golden light went from each to the other, and to all the rest, and back again, so the whole family was bound together in a nest of shining gold.

And Marley saw what the cord was; and he saw that he himself was a part of it; that the circle came from him, too, and returned, and that all were bound together.

The Cratchits were quiet after that, each alone with their thoughts, looking into the fire; each praying silently that they would all be together when the next Christmas came. Then it was time for bed; and it was a wonder to see the quiet way each of the children put aside their quarrels and differences, and made a point of carrying the littlest boy up, with many embraces and with kisses; they were children, and little devils, every one, but occasionally angels, too. After they had all been tucked in, and water gotten, Mr. and Mrs. Cratchit sat before the fire, her head on his shoulder, his arm around her waist. Then after a while, they went up to bed too, and Scrooge and the spirits were left alone in the room, watching the fire burn itself out.

"Spirit, will the littlest boy—the one with the withered leg—will he live?" asked the old man. The Spirit made his reply.

~

They were then on a wind-swept street. Cold and darkness and the wind, crying. Scrooge confronted the Spirit.

"Why do you show me these things," he demanded. "My life is nearly over—I'm too old to change. Go find some younger, better prospect. You torture me, you spirits, with your hope; but all your hope brings me is bitterness and pain. I'm old. Let me go."

"One thing more, old man."

~

And at the end, when the two skeletal children, the ravening, devouring figures of Want and Ignorance, crawled like roaches from beneath the Spirit's robe towards him, Scrooge was horrified, and screamed, and tried to get away—"have they no refuge, no resources?"—the Spirit replied terribly in his own words and vanished, mocking laughter filling the air.

Marley saw what Scrooge, his trembling fists covering his eyes, could not see: that when the Spirit that was Christmas Present departed, he took the two spectres, the two eternally starving, eternally dying children, and lifted them to his bosom; and, leaving the old man alone, carried them up and up, to the stars.

Scrooge stamped his bare feet on the cobblestones. "What am I supposed to do now?" he cried to the heavens. "You ask too much! I can't change! I'm too old!"

He shook his fists at the sky. "Might as well kill me!" he raged. "That would be more merciful!" He pounded on his chest. "Come on, take me! Take me away! Don't leave me here to ... "

Then he was gone.

Chapter Six

"**W**here did he go?" Marley was amazed. "What just happened?"

"I don't know," said the bogle, alarmed. "But we'd better find him. There's no time to waste—look." In the East the first gray light of morning was seeping into the sky. "Not much time left for us."

"Indeed," agreed Marley, and the two spirits flew off into the night.

~

A huge figure, robed in black, stood silent and unmoving at the foot of Scrooge's bed. The old man knelt before it, frozen in terror. For once he had no easy quips or sarcastic jabs; for some time he had literally nothing to say.

"Am I—am I in the presence of the Ghost of Christmas Yet to Come?" he finally forced out through trembling lips.

The shrouded figure did not move.

"You are about to show me the shadows of things that have not happened, but that will happen in the time before us?"

The figure inclined its head imperceptibly.

"Spirit, I fear you more than any spectre I have seen ... "

～

"Oh, Marley, this is wonderful!" The bogle was practically dancing with glee. "This is truly terrifying! I'm so proud of you! If this doesn't turn the trick, nothing will! Wherever did you get an idea like this?"

"I was about to ask you the same question." Marley stood beside him, watching the old man and the spectre.

"You mean that isn't you?"

"I thought it was *you.*"

"Well, if I'm here, and you're there, who is ... oh, dear."

～

"Will you not speak to me?" cried Scrooge. By now the old man was so frightened, and trembling so hard, that he could barely speak.

The grim phantom raised its arm and pointed a bony finger.

Scrooge swallowed hard and clenched his jaw, trying to stop his teeth from chattering. "Lead on, lead on, Spirit; the night is waning fast, and the time is precious to me, I know. Lead on."

The spirit took him away.

~

"There's only one Spirit that looks like that," said the bogle, "and you've seen Him before."

Marley nodded. His face was like a stone. "Has he come for old Scrooge, then?"

"It appears so."

"Then all of our efforts ... "

"Moot, now, I'm afraid."

"A waste of time," said Marley bitterly. "And they knew it when they gave him to us. We could never have really saved him. The game was rigged from the beginning!"

"Well, it seems to be over now," said the bogle, "and it looks like we've lost. Might as well follow them."

"I suppose."

~

So Marley and the bogle followed Scrooge and the Angel of Death on their final tour. The Angel showed Scrooge the effects of his absence; and the old man wept to see that no one cared. His housekeeper and laundress stole everything they could carry off; his office was closed for a respectable day or two, then reopened with Cratchit behind a much larger desk; his niece and nephew went to Paris to celebrate their inheritance; his funeral was unattended by any save the professional mourners hired by the undertaker to pad the bill. The spirit led the old man inexorably on, Scrooge becoming more and more desolate, until they arrived at a crowded, ill-kept graveyard crammed between some warehouses and a long-forgotten church. There was a place where the earth was fresh, and a cheap little headstone announced the final resting place of Scrooge's earthly remains.

"Poor old wretch," said Marley, as they watched Scrooge collapse onto his grave, burying his head in his arms, and weeping like an abandoned child.

"He asked for it," said the bogle. "He's got what he deserves."

"No one deserves—well, perhaps he does. Perhaps we all do. But no one ... " Marley left the sentence unfinished.

The old man crawled towards Death, weeping and begging and promising to change. "Spirit, hear me!" he blubbered. "I am not the man I was!"

"Poor old geezer," said the bogle. "Look at him beg. You could almost pity him."

Marley said nothing, but watched with an odd expression on his face. The figure of Death raised its arm, and the darkness behind him coalesced into a whirlpool of blackness—nothing, only black nothingness was visible inside. Death stepped to the edge of the vortex and held out his hand for Scrooge.

Marley stepped forward.

"What are you doing?" cried the bogle.

"I do pity the old booger," said Marley quietly. "Look at him—red-eyed, runny-nosed, pathetically begging for another chance. Let's give it to him." Marley raised his hand.

"What? But how—what are you going to do? You can't ... "

Time froze, and Marley was gone. Then, for the briefest instant, there were two Scrooges, mirror images, one kneeling in front of the other. "Old bastard," whispered the newer Scrooge to his astonished twin. "I never liked you before, and I don't like you any better now."

"Marley, don't do this!" cried the bogle. "You don't know what you're doing! You don't know what this'll mean!"

The duplicate went on, unheeding. "We all, every one of us, deserve a chance to change, a chance to do better," he whispered. "Here's yours." The double put his hand on the old man's chest and let it rest there, briefly, just above his heart. "Remember someone gave you another chance. If I can change, well ... " Then he shoved, hard, and one old man vanished; and when time began again there was just one Scrooge in the graveyard, kneeling before his Death.

"Marley, NO!" cried the bogle.

Thunder rumbled, and a high, keening wind arose. The Death-Angel hesitated for a moment, and lightning streaked the sky. Was it possible for a hooded face to show fury? The thunder roared as the Angel held out his hand to the duplicate Scrooge, and beckoned once more, savagely, demanding this time. The wind wailed about the old man, blowing his nightdress, blowing the wispy hair about his face. But he stood calmly, though he trembled a little; and calmly he walked to edge of the vortex where the Angel waited.

"Marley, don't do this!" cried the bogle, flying before his face. "No one's ever done this before. You don't know what it could mean! Annihila ... " The bogle's voice was lost in the shrieking of the wind.

The old man fixed the little spirit with one eye, and mouthed the word "Good-bye."

Then the old man put his trembling old hand into the Angel's outstretched one, and the two of them vanished into the blackness from which no man ever returns.

"MARLEY!" The bogle called and called, but he was alone in the graveyard. In the distance he heard the sound of a cock's-crow.

~

Scrooge awoke on the floor of his bedroom with a feeling of unreasoning joy. He wasn't sure where he was, or when he was, or even why he was, but he was glad that he was for the first time in a long, long time. He ran to his window. "Boy! What's today?"

"Today? Why, it's Christmas Day!"

The bogle watched the old man dance around in his underwear, giggling. The old man's good humor would have been infectious, had the bogle not been feeling a little lonely just then.

Suddenly Marley popped in beside him.

"Marley!" cried the bogle, leaping to embrace the old spectre's nose. "Where were you? Where did you go? What happened?"

Marley kept the little spirit in suspense for all of a second or two, then grinned and answered. "What could they do? I was already dead. Oh, there was a good deal of fuss, a lot of finger-wagging, and 'we shall have to deal with this very sternly at a later date, Mr. Marley.' I gather I'm in for it when we get back." He looked back at Scrooge. "Look at the old man dance!"

And Marley laughed aloud to see old Scrooge skip about as he dressed himself. The old man barely touched the floor, his happiness was so great. "I'm as light as a feather! I'm as happy as an angel! I'm as giddy as a drunken man!" Marley and the bogle laughed, sharing the old man's happiness. Then suddenly Scrooge fell to his knees.

"Jacob Marley," he said, to the air around him, "Heaven and the Christmas Time be praised for this! I say it on my knees, Jacob, on my knees!"

Marley found it difficult to speak for a second or two, and had to pretend he had gotten something in his eye. "Don't mention it, old thing," he finally said, his voice a little hoarse. "You're quite welcome, I'm very sure."

"I would call that 'a Complete and Willing Change of Heart,' wouldn't you?" said the bogle. Marley just nodded, having to clear his throat just then.

And the two followed Scrooge, dressed in his Christmas best—"Merry Christmas! Merry Christmas to you, sir!"—as he made his way to the counting house.

"What's going on?" said the bogle. "Surely he isn't going to work, today?"

"I don't know," said Marley. They didn't have to wait long to find out, for almost immediately the old man came running out of his counting house, his pockets brimming with coins of all denominations. He ran to the stone platform at the end of the street, and climbed the stairs, and then, standing in the middle of it, began to whirl like a dancer, casting the coins into the air like golden rain, and laughing and crying to the crowd that was beginning to gather, "A merry Christmas! God bless you! A merry Christmas to you, to all of you! There're a great many back payments in this, I assure you!" and the crowd laughed with him and blessed him right back, as they gathered the bounty; and not a hand left the square that day empty.

"You know," said Marley, as they watched Scrooge dancing down the street on his way to Christmas dinner at his nephew's, "I don't care what they do to us. I'm just glad we got it done. It's good to see him happy. And you know," he added, "I'm feeling pretty good myself."

"Me, too," said the bogle.

"Well, time to face the music?" said Marley.

"I believe so, old crumb-pot."

"They were pretty angry."

The bogle grinned. "Ah, hell's not so bad if the company's agreeable."

Marley smiled back at him. "After you."

"No, no, no. After you, I insist."

"Well, together then."

And the two spirits, the big one and the little one, disappeared into the Light.

Chapter Seven

Marley and the bogle, back in the celestial counting-house, stood before the record-keeper's desk. Still giddy from their experience on earth, they stood whispering and poking each other like schoolboys in the principal's office. The record-keeper sat behind the desk, frowning, his brow furrowed, looking over some documents, reports, by the look of them.

"Mr. Marley; we had said that you would be brought to account at a future time, and the various, um, *irregularities* of your behavior on the, um"—he checked the name—"Scrooge affair would be severely dealt with."

Marley and the bogle tried to stifle a laugh and failed miserably, most of it coming out their noses.

"Have I said anything funny? Would you care to share the source of your amusement?"

"No, sir—I mean, it's nothing, sir," said the bogle, before the two of them collapsed into helpless laughter.

"I see," said the record-keeper dryly. "You, sir, shall be dealt with first." His voice rang out with great severity and, suddenly, the two spirits before him were completely sober. "You were contracted, sir, to guide this soul on his journeys, and to oversee and shepherd his development. In that regard, sir," and here the record-keeper paused, frowning ferociously and glaring at the bogle through his spectacles, "in that regard, sir," he continued, despite the grin that now crept across his face, "you have acquitted yourself and your charge satisfactorily, and I am empowered to issue a promotion to you, sir."

With that, the bogle began to glow, then to shine, then to beam, then to blaze with a blinding white light. Within the light was no longer a pinched, severe little copy of Marley; a beautiful young man was in the center, or rather *was* the center of the light now, with lovely, big—yes—wings growing grandly out of his back.

"Thank you, sir," said the bogle, spreading his wings proudly.

"Not at all," said the record-keeper. He turned to Marley then, and for a moment Marley felt very small in the light of his eyes. Then the record-keeper smiled, gently. "Mr. Marley, you have fulfilled your contract admirably, as well, though your methods, sir, were highly unconventional. Still, as per the terms of your contract, 'all Debts are now Forgiven, all Bonds broken'"—

and here the shackles opened and the chains fell from Marley's hands, arms, waist, ankles, and neck—"'and the undersigned'—that's you, my dear sir—'shall be freed to seek his Greater Joy.'"

Marley raised his arms before him, showing the bogle that the chains were now gone. The bogle applauded and stamped his feet, whistling and cheering raucously, "Bravo, Marley, me darlin'!"

"Thank you," said Marley to the little spirit. "Couldn't have done it without you."

"A truer word was never spoke!" crowed the bogle. "Well, good-bye for now, m'dear! It's been grand!" He turned to the record-keeper. "Where do I go now?"

The record-keeper walked him over to a window that hadn't been there a moment ago, and pointed. "I believe it's somewhere about—there," he said, pointing up.

"I see it!" said the little spirit. "Well, I'm off! Keep in touch, old plum-pot!" And the bogle flew out the window, waving, "Good-bye! Good-bye!"

Marley hurried to the window, and waved back. He saw the light that was his friend go up, and up, and finally stop, and a new star shone in the eastern sky.

"Oh, my," said Marley.

"I know," said the record-keeper. "Never fails to move me, even after all these years. Well, sir, I wish you luck in your endeavors, and once again, congratulations on a job well done." The record-keeper shook

Marley's hand and went back to his desk.

Marley stood there for a moment. "Um, excuse me, but ... "

"Yes?"

"Where do I go now?"

"Why, wherever you please. You're free." The record-keeper returned to his work.

Marley felt a little lost. "Ah, yes. Well, thank you."

"Not at all."

Marley stood there a moment longer, and then walked to the door of the office, opened it, and stepped out. The door closed behind him. Before him, the universe was spread out, looking like the most beautiful starlit sky.

Marley stood there and looked at it for a long time. A long time. Then he sat down and looked at it for a long time. Then he got up, and turned once again to the door behind him, and knocked on it quietly.

~

"Yes?" came the voice from within.

Marley opened the door, and stuck his head around it. "If I may, sir?"

"Come in, Mr. Marley, come in. How may I help you, sir?"

"Well, I've been thinking, sir ... "

"Yes?"

"I've been thinking that, well ... " Marley stopped.

"Go on, sir, please."

"I was wondering—do you need any extra help? Around here? I was thinking that I enjoyed or, more precisely, I got more joy out of helping old Scrooge, and seeing him changed, and happy, than I can remember at any time in my life, and I was wondering if ... "

"Delighted, sir!" said the record-keeper. "Yes, of course we always have an opening for someone of your abilities. We were hoping you'd be interested! You've shown a marked talent, sir, for the work, most ingenious, and we admire your style of doing things."

Marley glowed a little, himself, as the record-keeper pumped his hand in welcome. He knew that he was Home, then—that he had found a home and a work that would keep him busy and happy for a long, long time.

"If you'll just step this way," said the record-keeper, leading Marley to the files. "I have a project that I'm sure you would find interesting, that could use some of your expert intervention ... "

But that's another story. May we all find our way Home, as Marley did, and the bogle did, and even old Scrooge did, finally. May our lives bring joy and light to those around us; and, like the bogle, may we bless the darkness as bright and shining stars.

And God bless us, every one.

THE

END

Tom Mula is an award-winning Chicago playwright, director, and actor. In 1991, he received two Joseph Jefferson Awards for Outstanding New Work and an After Dark Award for his co-authorship of *Sylvia's Real Good Advice*, the long-running hit musical based on Nicole Hollander's comic strip, and for his version of *The Golem* for the National Jewish Theatre. His notable roles include his award-winning one-man version of *The Circus of Dr. Lao*, Richard III, Caliban, Feste, and the Fool in *King Lear*. Mula has been Artistic Director of the Oak Park Festival Theatre for seven years, and teaches as an Artist-in-Residence at Columbia College. For the last five years he has appeared as Scrooge in the Goodman Theatre's production of *A Christmas Carol*.

Illustrator **Larry Wojick** lives in New York City where he has worked for sixteen years as a designer-illustrator for Tiffany & Company. This is his first book.